MODEEN:BLACK OPS

FRANK H JORDAN

ACKNOWLEDGMENTS

The situations, organisations, and characters in this book are fictional, and any resemblance to an existing or past entity is entirely coincidental.

This book is written in Australian English.

DEDICATION

To my beautiful wife

THE MISSION

Something's not right about this assignment

But how can Jo Modeen question orders from Beta team leader Ben Logan, a man she trusted with her life in the past and wouldn't hesitate to do so again? She must decide whether to follow her orders, or her instincts....
Realising their activities must be black ops even from NatSec, Modeen's team disperses under deep cover to unravel the web of secrets surrounding the mission, which takes them from country Victoria to Australia's national capital, and across the ocean to Kabul in Afghanistan.

CHAPTER ONE

Akeem Jibril took a long drag on his stogie and leaned back in his burgundy leather chair to exhale the smoke. Sucking his teeth, he ran nicotine-stained fingers over the hand-carved acanthus leaf trim and fluted columns of his recently acquired two-tone, double pedestal desk. Together with the matching hutch behind his chair, it gave his plush office an impressive executive feel, and made a stark contrast to the filth, poverty, and suffering visible through the richly-draped window of his building in downtown Kabul.

He took another nonchalant drag on his cigar and blew the smoke into the air above his head. Putting his feet onto the desktop and crossing his ankles, he held a mobile phone to his ear and listened for a few moments, and then frowned.

'Why him?' He spoke through meaty lips with a guttural Middle-eastern accent.

'He's our best chance of getting Akim released from prison.'

'But he is dangerous.' Jibril dropped his feet to the floor and sat forward to rest his elbows on the desk. 'Look at what he did to Batista's operation, the disruption to our plans.'

'Exactly.' The male voice on the other end of the call was emphatic. 'He has the resources to make this happen. And I know him, he will do anything to keep his family safe.'

'And when Akim is released, what makes you think this infidel won't come looking for us?'

'Leave that to me.'

At Jibril's acquiescent grunt, the phone went dead and he dropped it onto the desk. Leaning back in his chair again, his eyes narrowed as he sucked on the stogie and watched the blades of the ceiling fan slice pitilessly through the rising smoke.

———

On the outskirts of Melbourne, Australia, a dark-coloured van slowed to a crawl and pulled into the kerb fifty metres from a set of wrought iron security gates.

The driver switched off the motor and sat back to scan the broad driveway winding its way to a stylish house perched on a rise. The double-storey brick building was cleverly situated to capture views of the surrounding area, which was dotted with hobby farms and other homes on small acreages.

Inside the house, Emily Logan hummed a nursery rhyme as she lifted her baby from the soap-scented bath and wrapped her in a fluffy towel. The little girl gurgled, kicked her chubby legs, and reached up to tug at her mother's dark, professionally-braided locks.

Dropping a kiss on her round, pink cheek, Emily settled the baby on her hip and picked up her mobile. She pressed the contact marked 'Mum & Dad Logan' and propped the phone between her ear and shoulder as she made her way from the bathroom into the master bedroom, where she laid the chuckling baby on the king-sized bed.

'Logan,' a cultured female voice answered.

'Hi Mum.' As she spoke, Emily continued dressing her wriggling daughter. 'I've just finished giving Chelsea her bath so we'll be right over.'

'Hello love. We're all ready, and *so* excited about having our darling granddaughter for her first sleep-over. Is Ben picking you up from here?'

'No, I'm meeting him at the Hyatt.'

'I bet you're looking forward to your first "date" night since Chelsea was born?'

'Yes, but I feel a bit funny about leaving her for a whole night ... I hope she'll be good for you.'

'Of course she will! She's our little trooper, just like

her father. You two make the most of the night and enjoy yourselves. It's not often you get to attend a black-tie function and enjoy a night of luxury at the Hyatt.'

'Thanks Mum. Anyway, we'll see you soon.'

'Bye love.'

Emily tossed her mobile onto the bed and was busy putting the finishing touches to Chelsea's hair when the phone buzzed with an incoming call. She glanced at the caller ID. *Unknown.*

When she answered it, a deep voice said, 'Hi, Em. You on track?'

'Just putting a ribbon in Chelsea's hair, then I'll drop her off at your mum's.'

'Great, I'll wait for you in the Hyatt's main foyer. Give Chels a kiss for me. I've got one reserved for you when you get here.'

She giggled. 'I'll hold you to that.' Hearing her husband end the call, Emily slipped the mobile into her evening bag and hastened to finish her preparations, knowing it was an easy forty minute drive to the city from their five acre property in Macedon.

Slipping into the red off-the-shoulder evening gown Ben had bought her for the occasion, she stepped into a pair of patent leather high-heeled shoes and shrugged on a black cashmere snug. After deftly applying her makeup and giving herself a mist of Ben's favourite perfume, she took a quick, satisfied glance in the mirror, scooped her little girl into her arms and swept out of the room.

Taking care to lock up behind her as Ben kept reminding her to do, she tucked Chelsea into the baby seat of their Lexus sedan, and tossed a bulging bag decorated with pink elephants and lavender butterflies onto the back seat beside her. Sliding into the driver's seat, she pressed the remote control to open the roller door and put the key in the ignition.

The car's V8 motor growled into life and she eased out of the double garage. Nosing down the driveway, thinking with pleasure about the evening ahead, she pressed the second button on the remote and watched the wrought iron gates slowly part. Passing through them, she pressed the remote control again and stopped to make sure the gates closed behind her, once again thanks to Ben's constant reminders about security.

She took a quick glance in the rear-view mirror to check Chelsea's little fingers hadn't messed with her elaborate 'do'.

She wanted to look her best for the invitation-only banquet she and Ben were attending at the prestigious Hyatt Hotel in Melbourne's inner city. It had been a while since their last formal outing and Emily was looking forward to spending time rubbing shoulders with the dignitaries, not to mention a good dose of adult company.

She was still gazing into the mirror when a dark-coloured van screeched to a halt in front of her, blocking the path. She gave a start when four bala-clava-clad men carrying assault rifles jumped out and took up positions on either side of the Lexus.

Her eyes widened with fear.

She fumbled for the central locking switch on the driver's side door, and as all four door locks clunked reassuringly into place, she groped for her bag and phone.

Looking up, she saw the driver of the van leer at her as he pulled a pistol from his coat and made to get out of the vehicle. Her heart raced and adrenalin surged through her body.

Trying to recall Ben's instructions should she ever find herself in this situation, she dropped the automatic Lexus into drive and jammed her foot on the accelera-tor. The powerful motor roared and the car leapt forward.

The driver's leer vanished as he sprang back, folding his leg inside just before the Lexus slammed the door shut on him and rocked the van violently on its chassis. The impact crumpled its door and the sedan's front bumper.

The airbag in the Lexus deployed and threw Emily back in her seat. She kept the pressure on the accelera-tor, desperate to get away. Over the roar of the car's engine, the screech of metal against metal, the howl of the Lexus's smoking tyres and her own harsh breath-ing, she could hear Chelsea crying.

She sobbed through clenched teeth, 'It's alright, bub, we'll be alright.'

When the man standing closest to her smashed the driver's side window with the butt of his rifle, she flinched but didn't take her foot from the accelerator.

Cursing loudly, he reached in and ripped the key from the ignition, and then grabbed Emily by the hair and dragged her out of the car. Screaming, she fell to the ground but scrambled to get up, arms reaching desperately for the car, only to have a black cotton sack shoved over her head.

Bawling, 'No! No!' she felt a pair of strong arms lift her roughly and then she was thrown down, knocking the wind out of her. She gave a grunt and a cry of pain, but froze when she heard Chelsea's cries.

Moaning, 'My baby … my baby,' she reached up intending to yank off the sack, but was slammed backward by a blow to the head that left her gasping.

'Leave it on!' a man yelled in her ear. 'And shut up if you and your child want to live.'

Her head was swimming as she felt Chelsea being thrust into her arms. Clutching her whimpering baby tightly to her chest, Emily gulped and shuffled back into a corner as the van's side door screeched on its rails and slammed shut. She heard running footsteps outside and a door opening and closing, and then the driver yelled some instructions in a foreign tongue as the van lurched forward with a crunch of gears.

Two men remained standing on the driveway. They

watched the van speed away and then jumped into the Lexus. The driver tucked the deflated airbag back into the steering wheel's cavity, started the car, and with a smug grin at the man in the passenger seat, pressed the remote control. As the security gates opened, he put the car into reverse and backed it up the driveway and into the garage.

———

Ben stood in the Hyatt's foyer, head and shoulders above the crowd, frowning at the entrance. When his phone buzzed and vibrated in the inner pocket of his tuxedo, he automatically retrieved it and checked the caller ID.

Unknown.

Pressing 'Answer', he put the phone to his ear while his eyes continued scanning the main entrance doors.

'She's not coming, Ben,' a familiar male voice said calmly.

Ben's head jerked and then slumped as his heart pounded in his chest. With a tightening, white-knuckled grip on his phone, he muttered darkly in an uncharacteristically uneven voice, 'If she's harmed in any way….'

'Easy there, big fella,' the voice sneered. 'You do exactly as we say and you'll get them back in one piece, safe and sound.'

'Them? You took them both?' Ben winced when his question was met with a snigger. 'Why, Gator? If you've got issues with me, we can sort it out man-to-man. Leave innocent parties out of it.'

Suddenly aware someone had come to stand in front of him, Ben looked up to see Modeen. He raised a halting hand and turned his back to her. A second later he twisted his head to mouth at her, 'Five minutes.'

She nodded and walked off as Gator replied, 'Why? Because we need a level playing field. And you've been interfering with our plans.'

'By "we",' he said flatly, 'you mean the Spear of Allah.'

Gator chuckled. 'As always, you are well informed my friend.'

'What happened to you, Gator? Why are you doing this? The Gator I knew—'

'Stop wasting time! Don't forget what is at risk here.'

Grimacing, Ben pleaded, 'Let them go and I give you my word I'll do whatever you want.'

This met with a wry snort. 'I think we stand a better chance of having you do as we say with them right here. Oh, and we have you under surveillance so don't try anything rash or … you know how this goes. We have men stationed at your house and your work. In a moment a young lady will make contact with you. Give her your phone. She'll place a tracking device in it that will also monitor your calls. You are to keep it on you at all times. If anything happens to the phone or to any of our people, you won't see Emily or Chelsea again. Are we clear on that?'

'Yes … but—'

'You will receive further instructions once we know you are cooperating.'

His tone grew smarmy, but with a snide edge. 'For now you should go home, Ben. Do as we say and you'll get Emily and Chelsea back.' With a click, the phone went silent.

Ben took it from his ear and was staring at it when Catalina sidled up to him.

'Your phone please, Mr Smith.' Her crimson lips tipped upward in one corner and she purred, 'Or should I say Mr Logan?'

Ben stared at her, his eyes flinty slits as he passed her the phone. For a brief instant he thought about snapping her neck, but fear for Emily and Chelsea stayed his hand.

Flicking him a wary glance as though reading his mind, she opened the phone's leather cover and slipped a flat metallic device the size of a ten cent piece into an inner pocket. Pressing herself close against him, she slipped the phone back into his hand and smiled into his eyes. Murmuring throatily, 'We'll be tracking, watching, and listening to you at all times,' she backed away, still smiling, and sauntered off with a swing of her hips and a dismissive wave of her fingers.

• • •

Ben stood straight, stiff and silent in the chill of the night air, waiting for the valet attendant to retrieve his car. As soon as it pulled in front of him, he wrenched open the driver's door and yanked the valet out of the seat with a mumbled, 'Sorry mate, I'm in a hurry.'

Taking the driver's seat, he accelerated out of the driveway with a squeal of tyres, but promptly pulled into a parking bay on the road outside. After taking a quick look around to make sure he was alone, he pressed a button above the glove compartment and a twelve inch monitor emerged from the dashboard to unfold vertically in front of him. He placed his hand on the screen to log in and then tapped on a NatSec icon. A digital display representing a map of the world opened on the screen with blue and green dots scattered over it.

He entered 'TD93EM' into the search window and watched as the screen zoomed onto Australia, then Victoria, and finally onto a green dot bouncing along the Hume Freeway just south of Wangaratta. Ben sat transfixed on the screen, contemplating where they might be heading, but then snapped out of his trance and tapped the button above the glove compartment again. The screen folded back into the dashboard as his phone buzzed and vibrated with an incoming call.

His eyes narrowed as he put the mobile to his ear.

'Ben? Emily hasn't arrived yet. Is everything OK?'

He took a breath and struggled to keep his voice even. 'Sorry Mum, there's been a change of plans.

Emily isn't ... feeling the best so we've decided to give the function a miss. I'll call you tomorrow.' That was all he could manage, so he pressed End Call before his mother could question him further.

He sat back, his mind racing.

What would the Spear of Allah's demands be, and how would he get Emily and Chelsea back if he was truly being watched at all times?

Realising his stationary position might look suspicious to his observers, he threw the car into gear and sped away.

CHAPTER TWO

The lights were on in his house when Ben passed through the security gates. He peered at the house looking for movement as he drove slowly up the driveway and pressed the remote control to open the garage door. Nosing the car into its space, he was out within seconds and at the door connecting the garage to the house. Yanking it open, he took the three stairs in one long stride and marched into the kitchen.

The open plan home had high cathedral ceilings, and Emily had described its teak and granite kitchen as 'to die for' when she first saw it. But Ben's narrow-eyed focus was on the large, swarthy man sitting at the island bench, nursing an AK47 assault rifle.

Rising, the man squared his impressive shoulders, tightened his grip on the rifle and eyed Ben warily. 'Come in, come in,' he said in a thick Middle-eastern accent, 'I have been expecting you.' He indicated the laptop computer on the bench in front of him and grinned. 'It is good you came straight here. We have been monitoring your progress.'

Ben said nothing, merely fixed him with steely eyes as he slowly walked around the island bench to face him. Glancing at the laptop, he saw a white dot blinking on his current position on a Google Earth map.

The man pointed at the dot and sneered, 'We can track you at all times, do not forget that. And we have eyes and ears everywhere.' Shrugging, he spread his hands wide, making sure to keep a firm hold on the rifle as he did so. 'But where are my manners? I am Khalil, and as long as you do as we say you will see your loved ones again.' Keeping the gun's muzzle pointed at Ben, he cradled it in his dark, hairy arms and gave a malicious grin.

Ben's phone buzzed in his pocket and he turned to pull it out. Seeing the caller ID, he flicked a glance at a still grinning but now seated Khalil, and put the mobile to his ear. 'JD.'

'Where are you, Ben?'

Hearing the thread of anxiety in Modeen's voice, he took a deep breath before replying, 'There's been some dramas with the babysitter, and Emily's not feeling well. So I decided to come home.' He imagined her frowning, and could almost hear her mind working. He hoped she'd play it cool.

'You sound a bit stressed, Ben. Anything I can do?'

He snapped, 'No,' but then went on more calmly. 'Thanks. I've got some work issues I need to sort out. Anyway, why did you ring?'

'I got Leanne to run a check on Spooky's plus one, and it turns out she's Batista's niece.' He made no comment so she continued. 'I fronted her about it and she took off.' When he still didn't speak, her voice grew tentative. 'She's got a flat in Canberra, should I get Leanne to send the Feds over there to check it out?'

'I'll leave you to handle that, JD, I've got other things I need to focus on.'

'Alright ... but don't work too hard, you deserve a break.'

He ended the call with an abrupt, 'See you Monday morning,' and shoved the phone back into his pocket. Turning to Khalil, he growled, 'What is it you want me to do?'

'It is not for me to say, but rest assured you will be told in the fullness of time.'

Taking another step closer, Ben glared down at Khalil from his towering six foot four frame as the sound of footsteps behind reached his ears.

'This is Omar,' Khalil muttered with a lift of his unshaven chin.

Ben turned to see another swarthy man coming down the stairs at the far side of the lounge room. Scruffily dressed and with an unwashed look about him, he was also holding an AK47.

'As you see, you would be wise to mind your

manners,' Khalil said with a hint of triumph. 'If one of us does not report in every half hour, you will not see your family again. But you are free to move about the house. Just remember, we are here and will be watching you.'

Ben didn't speak as he strode through the lounge room past an awed-looking Omar, who kept his rifle trained on the big man. Climbing the stairs, Ben went into the master bedroom and sat on the edge of the bed. He looked down and fingered the fluffy pink towel with the little hollow where Emily had lain a freshly-bathed Chelsea mere hours before. Breathing in the lingering scents of baby powder and Emily's perfume, he gave an anguished groan and slumped forward, putting his head in his hands.

Hearing the two men downstairs laughing coarsely and making delighted noises as they raided his well-stocked fridge, he lifted his head with a sense of purpose and took out his phone. Tapping on an icon, he typed in TD93EM. The green dot on the screen had left the Hume Freeway and was heading along the Great Alpine Road toward the township of Bright in country Victoria. Ben sighed and flicked off the phone, taking a measure of comfort from the knowledge his wife and child hadn't been taken out of the state.

Yet.

———

When the van jolted to a stop, Emily heard the metallic screech and thud of a roller door closing behind the vehicle, and then the van's side door was flung open. Through the sack she caught a hint of low light as the van shuddered and a man climbed in beside her. She shrank back, clutching a sleeping Chelsea close, but he merely reached up from behind and removed the sack from her head.

Grabbing her by an elbow, the man ushered Emily out of the van and she squinted as harsh lights flickered on above them. In her arms, Chelsea murmured sleepily. Shading her baby's eyes, Emily glanced around. They were in what looked like a roomy garage with a double roller door. The walls were made of rustic brick and there was a narrow wooden staircase leading upward in the far corner of the room.

Shoved in the back, she stumbled toward the staircase. Risking a glimpse behind, she saw the dark-skinned man who'd smashed the window of her car and dragged her to the pavement.

'Quickly!' He prodded her between the shoulders with the butt of a rifle, jolting her forward.

She winced and began climbing the narrow stairs. At the top, a door opened inward and a distinctly Australian voice said, 'Welcome Emily.'

Seeing the tall, dark-haired man standing in the doorway, she stopped abruptly and took a double take. 'E-Eric?' she stuttered. 'But we thought you were missing in action?'

'You have a good memory,' he drawled, adding sourly, 'but you shouldn't believe everything you hear, especially from the military.' His eyes glinted and he gave a tight smile. 'It's been a while, but you're looking as lovely as ever.' Glancing down at the sleeping Chelsea in her arms, his smile wavered and he pressed his lips together. Taking one of her elbows in a firm grasp, he said pleasantly, 'Let's get you settled. Please, come with me,' and he ushered her up another flight of stairs.

'But ... I don't understand, Eric. What's this all about?' Emily's voice shook as she climbed the steps, staring up at him in bewilderment.

He opened a door at the top of the landing and led her into a good-sized bedroom with a queen-sized bed and an ensuite. A small bedside lamp threw soft light around the room under a lace-curtained dormer window, fitted with bars across the recess. The window itself was closed and locked.

Releasing his grip on her arm, he said, 'You should be comfortable in here.' He pointed to a bar fridge in the corner of the room on top of which sat an electric kettle, cups and an assortment of jars. 'There's tea and coffee in the corner. Let me know if there's anything else you need.'

'But Eric,' she said desperately, 'you haven't told me what's going on?'

Before he could answer, there was a rap on the door and one of the other men stepped into the room to drop Chelsea's overnight bag on the bed. When he left the room Eric made to follow him, but Emily put a hand on his arm.

'Eric—'

He half-turned toward her but didn't meet her eyes. 'Look, the sooner Ben does as we ask, the sooner you'll be home. That's all you need to know. Now just relax and take care of yourself and….' He frowned and lifted his chin toward the baby. 'Her.'

'Chelsea. Her name's Chelsea.'

He grunted and brushed her hand from his arm, before striding out and closing the door behind him. Emily stared after him and heard the door lock. She stood that way for a few seconds, before going over to try the handle just to be sure, only to find the door knob had been reversed so that the lock was on the outside.

With a sigh, she glanced around the room – her holding cell, she realised – and went over to the bed. After first inspecting the bedclothes, which she found relatively clean, she lay Chelsea down and pulled the baby bag closer. After changing Chelsea's nappy, Emily settled her drowsy little girl in between the pillows and then lay down, curling herself protectively around her baby.

She closed her eyes and bit back the sob rising within her. Glancing at her watch, she calculated that it had been a little over four hours since they'd been taken. In that time they could have made Albury to the north, or Lake Entrance in the east … or anywhere in between. She sniffed and wiped the tears from her face with her left arm.

Her left arm….

She gazed at it, remembering the piercing sting and her exclamation of pain. And in her head she heard Ben saying, 'Now, no matter where you are, I'll be able to find you.'

———

Ben was still sitting on the bed when his phone vibrated. His lips tightened and he placed it to his ear.

'You have two things to do, then you'll get your family back.' The voice was direct and to the point.

'You know how these things go, Gator,' Ben said flatly, swallowing his inner turmoil. 'Before I do anything I want proof of life.'

'Always by the book, hey Ben?'

'No.' He gave a wry snort. 'We wouldn't be talking right now if I were going by the book. You know we aren't supposed to negotiate with terrorists.'

'Well, I'm glad we have an understanding. And I wouldn't have expected anything less from you.'

Ben heard footsteps and a door creaking open.

'Is that you, Ben?'

At the sound of his wife's unsteady but hopeful voice, he winced and squeezed his eyes shut. 'Yes, sweetheart.'

'Oh Ben—'

He swallowed and said hurriedly, 'Are you OK? Have they hurt you or Chelsea in any way?'

'No, we're OK. Ben, Eric Crockman is here.'

'Yes, I know.'

There were some scuffling sounds as Gator took the phone off her, and then footsteps and the bang of a door closing.

'Right, you have your proof,' Gator barked. 'Now, for those two things I mentioned. First one is Harrison Baker. We don't want him replacing Andre Kane as the new Ambassador to Afghanistan. We don't care how you do it, just get rid of him.' He didn't wait for Ben to speak before going on.

'Secondly, we want Saddam Akim released from Parwan military detention facility in Kabul and delivered safely to us. The faster you get these things done, the faster you'll have your family back.' His voice grew low, threatening. 'And if you or any of your team try anything heroic, or we even *suspect* that you've spoken about this to anyone, the deal is off ... and you know what that means.' With a click, he was gone.

Taking the phone from his ear, Ben tapped on the icon and typed in TD93EM again. This time the green dot was stationary. He zoomed in on the location, and the image of a small acreage on Crystal Brook Avenue, Porepunkah, in country Victoria rose to meet him.

CHAPTER THREE

It was ten past eight Monday morning. Sitting in front of Ben's desk at NatSec HQ with Wolf, Spooky and Bugs, Modeen glanced at her watch and frowned. 'Ben's never late.' When her phone vibrated with an incoming call, she said, 'This might be him.' But when she looked at the caller ID, her frown deepened. 'Hi Dad, I'm just in a meeting can I call you back?'

John Modeen's voice was agitated. 'Josephine, I've found him.'

'You've found who, Dad?'

'The guy who was driving the car, the one who abducted me.'

She snapped to attention. 'What? Where?' At her sharp tone, the others eyed her expectantly.

'Here,' her father announced.

'WHAT?'

'No, sorry! Not *here* per se. I was transferring your old Army photos into the new album and I found him. It's definitely him.'

'But *who* is it Dad?'

'He's in a photo with you and the other soldiers. You wrote on the back of the picture "Afghanistan with Ben, Wolf, Spooky, Bugs and Gator".'

'Gator.' She blanched and sucked in a breath. Closing her eyes and then opening them again, she whispered, 'Oh no.'

'I saw the other four at the Hyatt on Friday night. This bloke was the only one missing.'

She didn't speak for a few moments.

'Josephine? You still there?'

'Yeah, Dad, I'm here.' She squeezed her eyes tight, swallowed, and forced herself to speak normally. 'Look, thanks for that, but I'd better go. I'll call you after the meeting.'

Clicking off the phone she turned wide-eyed and pale to the others, and was about to speak when Ben walked into the room and took his seat behind the desk. With a puzzled frown at his haggard appearance, she said without preamble, 'Ben, I've just received a call from my father. He's discovered the identity of his kidnapper.' She paused to take another breath. 'It's Gator. He's alive.'

Eyeing her wearily, Ben turned over a small stapled document that had been face-down on the desk and pushed it toward her with a finger. All four leaned forward to see what it was. 'ASIO Forensic Report' stood out in bold writing at the top of the cover page.

Modeen glanced questioningly at Ben, who finally spoke. 'That report confirms it. The fingerprints taken from the black 4WD that crashed off the Gillies highway....' Pausing, he ran a hand over his close-cropped hair before saying flatly, '... belong to Eric Crockman.'

The room went quiet.

Spooky was the first to break the silence, shaking his head in disbelief. 'No wonder I had trouble tracking him.'

'Gator's gone rogue?' Wolf too shook his head. 'Any leads on his whereabouts?'

'No leads,' Ben said, 'but now we know for certain he's associated with the Spear of Allah.'

Modeen eyed him. Something about the way he spoke made her think Ben was choosing his words carefully. But then didn't he always?

Bugs leaned his arms on the desk. 'He got away with being MIA for a good while ... but I guess we *are* talking about Gator.'

All five exchanged significant glances and nodded.

Ben turned to Bugs. 'I'm going to have to cut short your visit, mate. I need you back in Afghanistan ASAP.'

'Oh, man ... I was hoping to hang around for a while.'

Ben's brow creased and he said sternly, 'This is a priority mission, Bugs, and I expect you to perform to your usual high standard. Leanne has booked you on an Emirates flight that leaves tonight at nineteen fifteen. I'll provide you with all the details for your assignment as soon as I have them.' He turned to Modeen. 'I have your next assignment here.' He slid over a NatSec folder. When she glanced at it and then raised an eyebrow at him, he barked, 'What?'

'There's no event number.'

'Correct. We'll sort that out when the mission is completed. I want you to take Spooky and Wolf with you on this one, Josephine.'

Feeling like someone had scraped fingernails down a blackboard, Modeen flinched and shifted in her seat.

He called me Josephine … and why is there no event number?

Gathering her composure, she said, 'So, three of us. How many targets?'

'It's all in the folder. We need your target gone ASAP, and I want both missions....' Ben paused and looked at Bugs. '*Both* missions completed by nineteen hundred hours Wednesday.'

Modeen frowned at him. 'But that only gives us about seventy-two hours?'

'Correct.' Ben got to his feet. 'And you can only contact me on the mobile. I'll be working from home.' With a brusque nod in their direction, he marched out of the office.

The four agents sat back in their seats and shared a glance.

'Is this some sort of weird test?' a perplexed-looking Bugs enquired.

Wolf indicated the folder in front of Modeen. 'Let's head down to the mission room and go through the file.'

Modeen sat forward, picked up the file and tapped it on the desk, her expression a picture of concentration. Finally, she glanced at Wolf and said slowly, 'No. We'll go somewhere else. You're booked into the Rydges, Bugs?' At his nod, she said, 'Good, we'll go there and nut it out. That alright with you, Bugs?'

''Long as you don't mind a bit of mess – I wasn't expectin' visitors. Room 809, but give me five minutes, will ya? I wanna touch base with Leanne about my flight.'

Spooky sprang to his feet. 'I'll pick us up some coffees on the way. Meet you there.'

Modeen stood at the window of Bug's untidy – 'lived-in' according to its unapologetic occupant – motel room, gazing out at the impressive eight-floor view of Melbourne's inner city without seeing it.

Nearby, Bugs and Wolf sat around a small table, hands clasped behind their heads, staring at the open NatSec event folder like it was the spectre at the feast.

Nobody spoke.

They all still looked shell-shocked following the revelation about Gator.

At a knock on the door Modeen snapped out of her contemplation and went to open it, stepping over shoes, a damp towel, and Bugs' open duffle on the way. Spooky stood in the corridor holding four take-away coffees in a cut-out cardboard tray. Entering the room, he promptly distributed the hot drinks. 'Right-o, what's the deal?'

As though synchronised, all four whipped the lids off their cups and took grateful swigs of the hot, fragrant coffee.

It was Wolf who finally answered, drawling, 'Modeen's radar has shifted into overdrive.'

'The ever-present radar!' Spooky threw her a wink. 'Well I'm gonna follow that nose of hers. It's got us out of trouble on many occasions.'

Modeen eyed him levelly. 'Tell me, Spook, when have you ever been sent on a mission without knowing the event number?'

'Never.' He sat back in his chair. 'No event number, no mission. That's always been the rule.'

'Exactly.' A faraway look crept into her eyes. 'I reckon these missions are black ops. I doubt NatSec knows anything about them.'

Wolf glanced at her sharply. 'That's why you wanted us to meet here?'

'Yes. Until we know more, I think we should steer clear of HQ.'

Spooky frowned at her. 'What do you reckon is going on?'

'I don't know … and Ben's not saying.' She glanced around at the others. 'Did you see the dark circles 'round his eyes? It's like he hasn't slept for days. Then to top it off, in the meeting he called me Josephine.'

'Yeah,' Wolf muttered, 'I noticed that too.'

'Ben never does that,' Modeen went on, 'just like I never call him Sir.' Folding her arms, she paced the floor in front of them. 'You know, I felt something was wrong even on Friday night, at the banquet.'

Bugs sat forward. 'I must admit I've never heard Ben call you anything other than JD, but he might just be tired, like you said, not thinking straight.'

'What about the fact he wasn't interested in what we'd found out about Spooky's Catalina—'

'She's not *my* Catalina, thank you, not any more.'

'Sorry, Spook. But as I was saying, Ben's indifference struck me as strange and out of character.' Modeen tapped her forehead. 'What does it all mean?'

'It means he's got other priorities,' Bugs muttered, 'so somethin' big must be goin' down.' Seeing Spooky lean forward to grab the file and begin flicking through it, he said, 'That won't take you long. There's only one target, and there's not much info on him either. The initial background check suggests he's clean – no criminal record, no misdemeanours, not even a parkin' ticket.'

'Only *one* target?' Spooky looked mystified.

Modeen nodded at him. 'Yep, and that's another thing that doesn't feel right. Why would Ben send three of us on a one man op?'

'It doesn't make sense.' Wolf shook his head. 'And

did you guys notice that Ben said he wanted the target "gone"? He always uses the word "neutralised", never "gone".'

Spooky looked at Modeen. 'Who is the target?'

'Harrison Baker, due to replace Andre Kane as the new Australian Ambassador to Afghanistan.'

'Afghanistan?' Spooky frowned. 'Hey, you don't think Gator's got anything to do with this?'

Modeen looked at him sharply. 'Well, we know he's alive and working with the SoA, so it's possible he's in this up to his neck.'

'Oh, man!' Spooky threw his hands in the air and slumped back in the chair.

'I know Andre Kane,' Bugs said, 'he's a flea. I wouldn't trust him with Spooky's mother.' He dug Spooky in the ribs and was rewarded with an unimpressed huff. 'Maybe Kane's their puppet, and they want him to stay in that position.'

'But if Baker's eliminated won't they simply put in his understudy?'

'Good point, Spook. It'd be a good idea to find out who that might be.' Modeen turned to Bugs. 'You heard any more about your assignment?'

'Nah.' He dragged a hand through his strawberry blonde flat top and sucked his impressive set of teeth. 'We've gotta be missin' somethin'.'

Spooky sat forward abruptly and pointed to the inside cover of the file. 'Check out the pencilled-in small print there. What is TD93EM?' The other three leaned in for a closer look as he said, 'Am I right in assuming it's a tracking device?'

Modeen pulled out her phone and typed the string into her tracking app. It immediately zoomed in on a green dot.

'Well, whatever it is, it's in Porepunkah near Bright, about four hours north-east of here.'

Wolf narrowed his eyes. 'Could it be Harrison Baker?'

Spooky held up the file. 'According to this, Baker's based in Canberra. Besides, if he had a tracker fitted, I'd expect to see that fact highlighted here on the front page.'

Pulling out his phone and tapping on the screen, Wolf rose and walked to the window. 'So what's our plan?'

Modeen paced the floor. 'I think we should proceed as ordered.'

'Hey … this is interesting.' Wolf turned to face them and held up his phone. 'I've never been able to track myself or other agents before, only the devices I've activated and had the code for. And they've always shown up as blue. Now I've got four green dots in this building.'

He zoomed in on the dots and pointed to Modeen. 'TD9315'. Then he pointed to Bugs, 'TD9308,' and to Spooky, 'TD9307. And I'm TD9006 – I remember James telling me my number when he jabbed that freakin' tracker into my arm.' He looked thoughtful. 'But he said knowing the number wouldn't do me any good 'cos I wouldn't have the access authority to track myself, or other agents. Team leaders like Ben are the only ones able to do that.'

'Well,' and Modeen held up her NatSec mobile to show the same screen with the same dots, 'it now appears someone's seen fit to give us access privileges.'

As Bugs and Spooky pulled out their own phones to check, she said, 'I guess TD93EM must be another agent?'

Staring at his phone's screen, Spooky zoomed out for a complete map of the world and then zoomed back in again. 'According to this, TD93EM and the four of us are the only points of interest on the planet, besides one other green dot. TD9300 is moving up the highway toward Macedon, and I reckon that must be Ben, heading home.'

'I don't like it. If we're on the radar, who else is able to track us?'

'Relax, Bugs.' Modeen put a reassuring hand on his shoulder. 'Like Wolf said, access authority is restricted, and if Ben's granted it to us as well – on the quiet which I think is significant– we just need to figure out what to do with it.'

He sighed. 'So what *do* we do?'

Modeen stared at him for a long moment and then said, 'We stick to the plan. We may not know exactly what's going on, but we *do* know we can trust Ben. So it's off to Afghanistan for you, Bugs. As soon as you hear anything about your mission, let us know straight away. Wolf, I want you to check out TD93EM, it's the only tracking device we haven't accounted for.'

Wolf nodded.

'Spooky and I will go up to Canberra and check out Harrison Baker.' She turned back to Bugs. 'We're working on our own so we might need an extra pair of hands on this one. Do you think Salty would be interested?'

Bugs gave a toothy grin. 'Yeah, I reckon the old chowder-monger would be up for it. Whatcha got in mind?'

CHAPTER FOUR

'We need Salty to meet us at Spooky's apartment in Canberra ASAP.' Modeen eyed Bugs, and when he didn't move straightaway, she raised an eyebrow.

He found a new urgency and sprang to his feet. Reaching for his phone, he scrolled through the contact list for Salty's number while heading into the bedroom and closing the door. Behind him Modeen tapped on her phone and put it to her ear. 'Reece, I need you to book three flights on the next available plane from Melbourne to Canberra. For Troy Ryan, Luke Williams and me.'

There was a short pause.

'Right, Qantas from Tullamarine in ninety minutes. Thanks.' She ended the call.

'*Three* flights to Canberra?' Wolf raised a questioning eyebrow.

'Until we know what's going on, it has to appear to everyone – and that means everyone at NatSec as well – that we're following orders to the letter.'

'Ahh yes … black ops,' Spooky murmured as Bugs came back into the room.

'Did I hear right? We're on black ops?'

Modeen gave a grim nod. 'But on the surface it'll appear that we're simply following orders.'

'Right than.' Bugs was clearly unfazed at the prospect of going deep undercover. 'Now, Salty reckons he can be at Spooky's apartment by nineteen hundred hours tonight. In the meantime, do you want me to go with Wolf?'

She shook her head saying firmly, 'No. It's an eight hour round trip to Porepunkah and back, that'd be cutting it too fine. You could end up missing your flight to Kabul and we can't risk that. For some reason Ben needs you over there, so we shouldn't deviate from those orders.'

———

A bright-eyed young man sat in a back corner booth of a trendy café in Melbourne's CBD. Snappily dressed in a smart business shirt and tie, long pants, and black shoes with fashionably elongated toes that extended well past his own, he sat watching the café's milling clientele, his eyes peeled for someone. When a curvaceous brunette pushed her way through the crowd and slinked toward the booth, he gave a delighted smile, running his eager eyes over her figure-hugging blue denim jeans and knee-high black boots.

She leaned in to drop a kiss on his forehead, skilfully deploying the plunging V-neckline of her tight-fitting T-shirt in the process. Brushing crimson-tipped fingers over his jawline, she squeezed into the booth next to him and reached under the table to slip a small paper sachet into his waiting hand.

Putting an arm around him she pulled him in close, saying in a sultry purr, 'Anything to report?'

He raised his eyes from ogling her cleavage to give her a sideways glance. 'Only that he came in this morning for a meeting with the four of them, and then left the building about ten minutes later. One of the four is flying to Kabul tonight, and the other three have booked flights to Canberra.'

'Good boy.' She reached a hand under the table to squeeze his leg and put her plump, glossed lips close to his ear. Her breath was hot against his skin when she whispered, 'I'll see you tonight, same time, same place.' Giving his thigh another squeeze, she slid out of the booth and made her way through the queue of customers at the café counter, leaving him breathing in the heavy musk scent she left in her wake.

Stopping at the café entrance, she turned and blew him a kiss, before stepping onto the pavement and disappearing into the city bustle.

The young man slipped the sachet she'd given him

into his top pocket. Leaning back in the booth with his hands behind his head, he licked his lips and gave a lascivious grin.

———

When Wolf barked, 'Pull over here!' the turban-headed taxi driver nearly jumped out of his skin. He braked hard and swung the Black and White taxi tight against the kerb.

As Wolf got out, Modeen buzzed down the front passenger's window and looked up at him with a smile in her eyes. 'Take care.'

'Good luck, Wolfman,' Spooky called as he slid across to the spot Wolf had just vacated.

Throwing them a lazy salute, Wolf muttered, 'Catch you on the flip-side.' He watched the taxi pull out onto Mount Alexander Road and continue toward Tullamarine airport. Then he turned to gaze at the huge car yard in front of him. The sales office, sporting the sign *Essendon North – New and Used Cars*, was situated at the far end of the massive yard.

Wolf grunted.

Hope this guy's got insurance.

Strolling along the front of the yard, he mused, *Hmm … what'll it be … a Honda Accord, VW Golf, or the big black Chrysler V8 sport?* His primal instinct drew him to the V8, but his head told him to take the Golf. It wouldn't attract as much attention. It was also parked conveniently close to the exit driveway, and was finished in a nondescript silver duco that would blend in.

Stepping over the low chain barrier at the front of the yard, Wolf looked through the car's window. Seeing the keys dangling from the ignition, he gave a satisfied snort.

Just as I ordered.

Opening the driver's door, he pulled the *For Sale – test drive today!* banner off the windscreen, slid into the driver's seat and turned the key in the ignition. The little hatch started with an obligingly quiet purr, and he wasted no time easing it off the driveway, checking the rear-view mirror as he did so.

They probably won't even know it's gone 'til they do a key count tonight.

Accelerating and quickly merging into the traffic, he leaned forward to turn on the radio and tapped the GPS icon on the touch screen. Typing in 'Porepunkah', he tapped 'go'. A robotic female voice announced, 'Estimated time of arrival at destination, three hours and twenty-eight minutes.'

Glancing down at the fuel gauge, he swore under his breath.

This thing's runnin' on vapour, what a bunch of cheap-skates. I'll take my business elsewhere in future. He gave a wry snort and then frowned. *I'd better stop for fuel, ASAP.*

. . .

Arriving at Tullamarine, Modeen and Spooky made their way to the check-in counter to collect their tickets. On the way, Modeen reached up to tousle her blonde hair and undid the top button of her shirt.

Leaning over the counter to smile at the male attendant, she said throatily, 'Bennet and Williams, flying to Canberra. I'm afraid our travelling companion, Troy Ryan, isn't able to make the flight.'

The attendant didn't look up as he said flatly, 'These are non-refundable tickets.'

'Oh, I understand.' Modeen kept smiling, and this time she was rewarded with a glance, a double-take, and then an admiring smile in return. 'I just wanted to let you know he won't be making the flight, so there won't be any hold-up,' she said sweetly, 'and to save you having to contact the booking agent.'

'Why thanks, ma'am, that's thoughtful of you.' The attendant dragged his eyes away from her smiling china blue ones to tap on his keyboard. A few seconds later, he handed them their tickets. 'Gate twenty-three, boarding at eleven fifty-five.' He threw Modeen a wink. 'I gave you exit row seats. Have a good flight.'

As they made their way through security, Spooky muttered, 'It's so easy for you women, isn't it? You just smile your little smiles and blokes are putty in your hands.'

'We didn't make the system, Spook, we just use it. And you've gotta admit, it gets results.'

He merely grunted in response.

At gate twenty-three, they dropped their bags beside an empty row of seats and sat down.

Tilting his head toward Modeen, Spooky said quietly, 'We're not going to whack this guy, are we?'

'Let's just say I'm leaving our options open 'til we're sure we know what's going on.' She threw him a smile.

Taking out her phone, she entered 'Harrison Baker' into a Google search window. A formal family photo appeared, the same one that was in the NatSec file.

It featured a clean-cut middle-aged man in a black suit flanked by his wife in a heavily-laced evening gown, her hair up in a bun. Beside them their two children, a boy and girl, appeared to be around ten and twelve years of age. Gazing at the snapshot, she said thoughtfully, 'If things pan out the way I expect them to, we're definitely going to need Salty.'

Spooky looked over her shoulder at the photo. Taking care to keep his voice low, he murmured, 'Baker certainly doesn't look like your typical player.' He sat back. 'By the way, what do you know of Salty's background? How does he know Ben?'

'He's a good friend of Ben's dad, apparently. I only had a brief chat with him last Friday night, but from what I can gather, Richard Salt is a retired ASIO operative. His career included spending time in the US working with the CIA.'

'Do you think we can trust him? I mean *really* trust him?'

'Well, he was the one who alerted us to the where-abouts of the trawler on our last mission. Without his intel....' She bit her lip and continued. 'Bugs and Ben certainly trust him, and if he's OK by Ben, he's OK by me. Besides, I have a sneaking suspicion that Salty might've had a hand in Ben joining NatSec in the first place.'

A nasal voice issued from the ceiling-mounted speakers above them. 'Passengers on Qantas flight Q1538 to Canberra, your flight is now boarding through gate twenty-three.'

Rising to their feet, Modeen and Spooky joined the queue forming in front of the gate. Tapping on her phone, Modeen placed it to her ear and heard a deep voice answer, 'Ryan.'

'We're about to board the plane. Give me a call as soon as you know anything.'

'Copy that. ETA two hours and fifty five minutes.'

'Good, we should be back on the ground by than, and will hopefully have some more info on Baker. Oh, and Wolf?'

'Yep?'

'When you know for sure who 93EM is, call me. And stay out of sight, we don't want to attract atten-tion or tip off anyone.'

'Affirmative.' Pausing, he said gruffly, 'Look after yourself, Ms Bennet.' He ended the call and pulled off the Hume Highway into a BP service station at Wallan. The low fuel warning light on the Golf's dashboard had been flashing urgently for the past fifteen minutes.

Great, it's got a Maccas. At least the coffee here should be reasonable.

CHAPTER FIVE

Stepping off the Boeing 717 at Canberra airport, Modeen and Spooky headed straight to the long term parking and retrieved his black NatSec Aurion.

Fastening her seatbelt, she glanced across at him settling into the driver's seat. 'Do you know how to get to Baker's building from here?'

'Yeah, I know where Defat is. This is my town, remember?'

She looked at him blankly. 'Defat?'

'You know, the Department of Foreign Affairs and Trade, DFAT.'

'Oh, right.' She rolled her eyes.

'They're situated in the Richard Casey Building on John McEwen Crescent in Barton. Right next to Capital Hill, where all the knobs hang out.' Spooky paused, and then said thoughtfully, 'If we take Morshead Drive and then Kings Avenue it should only take us about ten minutes.'

'Will we go past a workwear store by any chance?'

'No, but there's a couple over Fyshwick way. What're you thinking?'

Busy doing a Google search on her mobile, she mumbled, 'I'd like to pay Baker a visit in his office but I'm going to have to look a bit more corporate. If you know what I mean.' She gave him a sideways grin.

'Fyshwick it is.' Nudging the Aurion forward, Spooky swiped his credit card at the boom gate and then headed out of the carpark and onto Pialligo Avenue. After a few minutes of confidently negotiating the traffic, he pulled up in front of a workwear store in Barrier Street. As the car rolled to a stop, Modeen got out and disappeared inside the shop.

When she emerged fifteen minutes later empty-handed and got back into the car, Spooky tilted his head at her. 'No good?'

'We've got half an hour to kill. They're just embroidering some logos for me.' She glanced at her watch. 'How about we get something to eat?'

'Sounds good. There's a great little pub just around the corner.'

———

'Modeen.' Bugs' voice on the phone was urgent, and echoed like it was coming from a deep place. 'I've just had a text from Ben.'

'And?'

'My assignment is to escort one Saddam Akim out of a US military prison in Kabul. Ben's informed the Americans that we're taking Akim to an ASIO safehouse, under the guise of interrogating him in relation to the Spear of Allah events in Oz.'

Modeen frowned. 'What do you mean "under the guise"?'

'Here's the kicker. Akim won't be going anywhere near the safehouse. Ben has instructed me to hand him over to the SoA.'

'What?' Her voice rose. 'The US army won't stand for that! And what makes Ben think he'll be able to get him released into your custody in the first place?'

'Salty helped him with that apparently. The old dude still has some pretty influential contacts within the CIA. And I don't think the US army's expectin' to get Akim back, if ya catch my drift.'

'I see.'

'Anyway, Salty'll be able to tell you more when he gets there.'

'Did Ben send you an email with the event number and details?'

'No, just a text, and still no event number. It seems like he's doing everything by phone. He's gonna send another text shortly with details of the prison pick-up and the drop-off location.' Bugs paused. 'Reckon this one's off the NatSec radar too, Modeen.'

'Hmm.' She stopped to think and then said, 'Have you got someone you can trust in Kabul? Someone to lend you a hand?'

'Sure, that shouldn't be a problem. What've you got in mind?'

After going over the plan with Bugs, Modeen ended the call. She turned to Spooky, who'd just popped the last portion of steak sandwich into his mouth. At her nod, he set down his cutlery and rose, still chewing, to follow her out.

Back in the car, they returned to the workwear store. This time when Modeen emerged, she was wearing navy blue trousers and a pale blue pinstriped blouse. Pausing on the footpath, she surveyed the surrounding shopfronts and then turned and strode a few doors up to a party hire business.

Spooky nudged the car forward and minutes later gave a wolf whistle as a shapely, long-haired brunette slipped into the passenger's seat. He grinned. 'Nice wig, and since when have you needed glasses?'

When she threw a plastic bag containing her old clothes onto the back seat, he spotted the label embroidered above her left breast pocket. 'I see you're with WorkSafe ACT, ma'am ... very impressive.'

'Let's hope it gets me into his office.' Pushing the stylishly framed costume glasses on top of her head, Modeen took out her NatSec ID card and clipped its lanyard to the waistband of her new trousers, making sure the card faced inward. Then she opened the glovebox and pulled out a small black case which she opened on her lap.

Three tiny tracking disks rested snuggly in a foam recess at its base, below an electronic device. She removed one of the disks and placed it into the cradle of the device. When she pressed 'activate', the device's LED screen flashed 'TD6020' and then 'Activated'.

Taking out her phone, Modeen checked her tracking app, slipped the glasses down over her nose and turned to Spooky. 'Right, time to pay Mr Baker a visit.'

Turning off John McEwen Crescent into Sydney Avenue, Spooky eased the Aurion onto the semi-circular driveway at the south-west side of the Richard Casey building.

Modeen waited until the car stopped moving before stepping out onto the sidewalk in front of a glass-roofed portico.

Inside the complex, the collection of multi-storied buildings sprawled across an entire block. Its central structure was flanked by two symmetrical wings on each site, making the facility look more like a modern day castle than a government building.

'Let me know if you need a hand.' Spooky held up

his phone with the screen facing her. 'At least I'll be able to track where you are in the building.'

Modeen touched two fingers to her temple in a casual salute before turning to walk with purpose through the portico and along a sheltered pathway to a large, leafy atrium. Continuing through the atrium, she reached the central main foyer and stopped in front of an electronic directory.

When she entered 'Harrison Baker' on the touch screen, a map showing her location appeared. The display read 'Elevator four, level three' and indicated the lift doors directly in front of her. She pressed the button for the elevator and a second later the doors opened with a discreet swish. Stepping inside, she swivelled to stare impassively outward as the doors closed again. After a brief and quiet ride upward she arrived at level three.

Stepping out of the lift, she took a quick glance to the left and right and saw that the corridors stopped at heavy security doors with swipe-card locks. Directly in front of her was a marble-topped reception counter encased in security glass.

When the mature-aged lady manning reception looked up, Modeen said pleasantly through a small window in the glass, 'Hello. Josephine Bennet to see Harrison Baker.'

The receptionist eyed her sceptically. 'Do you have an appointment?'

'No, I don't.'

'Well then I'm afraid that's not going to be possible. But I can book you in for another time, say next week?' She tapped on a keyboard.

Modeen took a step back from the counter. 'I'm a Senior Inspector with WorkSafe ACT.' She flashed her ID, taking care to cover the NatSec logo with her index finger, and then let the card promptly snap back on the lanyard reel. 'I understand Mr Baker will soon be relocating to Afghanistan.'

She raised her eyebrows and when the woman made no move to contradict her, she went on. 'Before he leaves, I need to go over with him the department's policies and procedures in relation to overseas deployment.'

'But—'

Moving nearer, Modeen spoke directly into the little window. 'This *is* a workplace and I *do* have authority to enter, but I'd prefer to do this amicably.'

'All this for policies and procedures?' The receptionist regarded her over her horn-rimmed glasses.

Modeen could see the woman was beginning to grow flustered and gave a lofty smile. 'I don't want to cause a fuss, but it *is* important. And I only need ten minutes of his time.' When she was greeted with an uncertain silence, she sighed. 'Or I can have Security escort me to Mr Baker's office....'

'One moment, please.' The receptionist put the desk phone to her ear and turned her back. When her call was answered, she lowered her voice but not so much that Modeen couldn't hear. 'I have an Inspector from WorkSafe here.' The woman paused and then clicked her tongue. 'Yes … but she says it's important.' She paused again. 'Right.'

Hanging up, she turned back to Modeen and said stiffly, 'Please take a seat. Mr Baker will see you shortly.'

Five minutes later an officious-looking young woman dressed in high heels and a figure-hugging business suit appeared through the security door to Modeen's right.

As she approached, Modeen rose to meet her and the young woman eyed her up and down unashamedly.

Small frog, Modeen sniffed to herself, *big pond.*

Stopping in front of her, the administration officer said haughtily, 'Please follow me.' Spinning on her lofty heels, she went back the way she had come, swiping her security pass at a series of doors along the way.

When they entered a large open plan office, Modeen glanced around at the work stations which were separated by low, sound-retarding partitions. Overhead, funky single-blade ceiling fans circulated air from the discreetly situated air-conditioning ducts.

The young woman continued on to the far end of the office and stopped at a closed door marked 'Harrison Baker'. She gave a peremptory knock before opening the door and announcing, 'The WorkSafe Inspector to see you, Mr Baker.'

Modeen didn't look at her as she brushed past and entered the office, to see a middle-aged executive type rise to his feet straightening his charcoal-grey suit.

Harrison Baker surveyed her appraisingly and then extended a hand, which she promptly shook.

'Senior Inspector Josephine Bennet.' As she spoke, she heard the office door being closed behind them and the click clack of high heels stalking away.

'Pleased to meet you, Ms Bennet.' Baker indicated a chair in front of his desk. After they were both seated, he threaded his fingers together and regarded her over them. 'Now what can I do for you?'

Modeen could see from his shrewd gaze that this was no fool. She would need to be quick on her feet if she wanted to keep up the charade … and make him believe it. She took care to mirror his attitude of casual interest. 'Thank you for seeing me, Mr Baker. It's your upcoming deployment to Afghanistan that I'd like to talk to you about.'

'Oh yes?'

'I've been asked to go over the policies and procedures the Department of Foreign Affairs and Trade has in place to ensure the safety of their employees. In particular, I'm interested in the overseas induction process.'

He gazed at her levelly from across his expansive corporate desk. 'I'd be happy to provide a copy of our procedures and policies, and can assure you the documentation is comprehensive. As I'm certain you're aware, the health and safety of our employees, especially those posted to regions such as Kabul, is paramount.'

Modeen nodded as he continued. 'Is there any specific area within the induction process you want to focus on?'

She held his gaze. 'We prefer to take a holistic rather than a task-specific approach to safety, Mr Baker.'

'Please call me Harrison.' He smiled and she realised he was younger than she'd first assumed.

'Thank you.' She pulled a notebook out of her top pocket and flipped it open. Pretending to scan the blank page, she said, 'So, Harrison, having written policies and procedures is important in an organisation this size, but they're worthless if not followed out in the field.'

Snapping the notebook shut and slipping it back into her pocket, she raised her eyes to meet his.

'Which means they should be readily available to all staff and must be updated regularly to cater for organisational and business changes.' Her mind raced, trying to recall what she'd read in her quick bone-up on the WorkSafe website. 'And of course they need to be enforced.'

'Of course.'

She warmed to her subject. 'Let's take the recent

outbreak of Ebola. In light of that, I would expect to see stringent controls in place for people travelling to and from infected regions.'

Baker nodded and sat back, eyeing her with new respect. 'I appreciate your concerns, Ms Bennet.'

'Please, call me Jo. And while they're my concerns, they should also be yours. Safety is everyone's responsibility.'

'Yes, of course, Jo. But I wonder if perhaps you'd be better off discussing this with our safety people?'

'That won't be necessary, for now. While I'm sure they're well versed in the policies and procedures, in fact, they probably wrote them,' to which Baker gave a sheepish grin, 'as you're the person being deployed it's your understanding of them that I'm most interested in.'

He gazed at her, and Modeen knew he was expecting some action from her. She sat forward. 'However, to start with I'd appreciate your emailing me that copy of your policies and procedures? By the end of the week would be fine.'

'Certainly.' Baker looked faintly relieved and picked up a pen and a bright yellow Post-it notepad. 'Your email address?'

'Josephine Bennet....' She searched her mind for an appropriate email address, knowing he would expect the government format. '... at WorkSafe dot ACT dot gov dot au.'

He scribbled it down. 'I'll have them sent by close

of business today. Now, is there anything else I can help you with?'

'Just one detail. Could you tell me what the department's contingency plan would be, say … if you got sick and couldn't make it to Afghanistan?' She was careful to keep her tone casual and business-like.

'Well of course that would be the department's decision, but I believe they would either leave Mr Kane in the position for an extended period, or install my protégé, a bright young chap named Ivan Singh.' Baker smiled indulgently.

'I see. Well, it's good to know the department has some controls in place to manage such contingencies.'

Rising to her feet, she extended a hand and he rose to shake it. 'Thank you very much for your time, Harrison.'

'My pleasure, Jo. Don't hesitate to let me know if you need anything else.'

She smiled and her eyes fell on his briefcase. 'Say, that's a lovely case.' Reaching out a hand, she ran her fingers over the rich leather binding. 'Is it crocodile skin?'

'Yes,' Baker said proudly. 'An anniversary present from my wife.'

Her eyes alighted on the far corner of his desk, where a familiar family picture sat in a pewter frame. She gave a smiling nod. 'Thanks again for your time.'

'Good day.' Baker was already taking his seat again as she stepped out of his office.

Going back out through the security doors and passing by the reception desk, she waved and mouthed, 'Thank you,' at the receptionist before stepping into the elevator. Once back on the ground floor, she strode out of the main entrance onto John McEwen Crescent, and was pleased to see Spooky pull up in the car as she got to the kerb.

CHAPTER SIX

Turning right off the Hume Highway, Wolf took the third exit into the tiny township of Porepunkah at the foot of Mount Buffalo. The vivid autumn foliage, rolling hills and tranquil rural setting filled him with a sense of calm. But that made him frown.

Snap out of it, he chided himself irritably. *Next thing I know, I'll be listening to Justin Bieber.*

He gave a bemused snort and checked the GPS, before turning into leafy, tree-lined Crystal Brook Avenue. The narrow lane fronted a string of small acreages on his right, separated from each other by stands of forest.

Slowing the car, he passed two properties of fenced grazing land and then came to the first house. Grabbing his mobile, he checked the tracking app.

The green dot of TD93EM was parallel to his location, approximately fifty-five metres in from the road.

Peering up the driveway, he made out the apex of a roof through the trees.

He didn't stop. Continuing along the avenue he eyed the neighbouring house, an imposing double-storied red brick with a stark symmetry that looked out of place in the countryside's gentle curves and rolls. The next property along the road had a For Sale sign attached to the front fence.

Coming to a stop just before its driveway, Wolf stared in at the low-set residence. It looked freshly painted and landscaped, and – most importantly – unoccupied.

With a quick look around to see if anyone was watching, he drove the Golf through the gate and up the driveway. Parking in the lee of the house, he switched off the ignition and sat back, listening.

The only sounds to greet him were bird calls, a dog barking in the distance, and the gentle gurgling of a nearby stream.

Reclining the seat and crossing his brawny arms over his chest, he settled in to wait for darkness to fall, thinking sourly, So now it's hurry up and wait, just like in the army….

———

Spooky looked up as Modeen slid into the passenger's seat. 'How'd you get on?'

She took off the glasses and rubbed the bridge of

her nose. 'I've scoped the building and confirmed our intel on Baker, and I discovered an interesting little snippet.'

'Oh yeah?'

'If he weren't able to take up the Ambassadorship, it's possible Baker's protégé, one Ivan Singh, might step into the breach.'

'Ivan Singh?' Spooky frowned. 'Sounds like a cross between a Russian and a Middle-easterner. That's a dangerous combo if you ask me.'

Fixing him with a level gaze, she mused, 'On the other hand, he might only be as dangerous as the next up-and-coming politician. But we'll know you're right if he pulls an AK47 or Type 56 on us.' She fastened her seatbelt as Spooky started the car. 'I'd like to run a background check on him but we can't involve NatSec, so it'll just have to wait.'

As they pulled away from the kerb he threw her a glance. 'So, what's our next move with Baker?'

She looked thoughtful. 'There are too many security cameras and locked doors in that place for my liking. We're better off grabbing him in transit, on his way home.'

Holding up her phone, she indicated the screen. 'I planted TD6020 so we can track him. We'll hang around and grab him when he leaves the office. But first we need to find a chemist, and I'll have to borrow your Glock.'

'Sure.'

'And then it's just the usual, hurry up and wait.' She grinned and gave his shoulder a fist bump.

He muttered, 'Now I *know* we're back in the army,' and accelerated into the traffic.

When the clock in Harrison Baker's office struck four-thirty, he glanced at his watch to confirm the time. Shuffling papers together on his desk, he bundled them into a folder which he slipped into his briefcase. He clicked the locks, lifted the case and rose to his feet. Turning out the light in his office, he closed the door behind him and made his way through the now deserted open plan office and down to the executive carpark. He was used to being one of the last to leave. Most of the other officers finished work at four pm, and were disinclined to work past their knock-off time.

As he strode through the front entrance of the main building, he was mulling over a report he had to present to his superiors and pondering where to buy a bunch of roses for his wife on the way home.

Unaware that someone was closing in fast behind him, he turned left and headed to a white government-issue sedan. As he approached the car he clicked the remote to unlock it. Opening the back door, he tossed his briefcase onto the seat, and then removed his suit jacket and laid it flat on top of his briefcase. After shutting the door, he moved forward to the driver's seat and slid behind the wheel. To his surprise, Modeen slipped into the passenger's seat next to him.

Startled, he jerked back and then took a double take. 'Hey, it's you, the safety lady.' He stared at her stunned, and then collected himself, narrowing his eyes reproachfully. 'Say, your email bounced.'

Her lips twitched at his reaction, but she had the courtesy to look chagrined. 'Yeah … sorry about that.'

Seeing her glance down significantly, he followed her gaze and sucked in a sharp breath. She was holding a pistol low, aimed at his abdomen. The thick, four inch silencer attached to the Glock's barrel made it look even more imposing. When he looked up again, she saw fear in his eyes.

'You're not with WorkSafe are you?'

'What gave me away?' She gave a crooked grin. 'Look, if you do as I say, you won't get hurt. Now start the car.' When he sat motionless in his seat as though frozen, she prodded him with the muzzle of her weapon. 'Don't think, Baker, just do it.'

He snapped out of his trance and turned the key in the ignition, casting furtive glances at her as he did so.

'See that black Aurion over there?' With a lift of her chin she indicated Spooky's car parked on John McEwen Crescent.

Baker swallowed and croaked, 'Yes.'

'I want you to follow it.'

He took a breath and faced her. 'Look, what's this all about?'

'Just do it.' She prodded him again with the muzzle of the Glock.

'OK, OK.' His hands were unsteady on the wheel as he reversed the car out of the space and drove it out of the carpark.

As they approached, the Aurion moved slowly away from the kerb to allow Baker to pull in behind it. The two cars entered the circular ring road around Capital Hill and took the exit onto Adelaide Avenue. A short time later they took another exit onto Yarra Glen, then Melrose Drive and finally Devonport Street. The Aurion pulled off the road and bowled down a gravel track that led behind a high voltage power substation.

Baker looked around the isolated spot. 'W-what are we doing here?' His voice shook.

'Pull in behind the other car, turn off the engine and hand me the keys.'

He did as he was told, his hand visibly shaking as he passed over the keys.

'Good. Keep doing as I say and you won't get hurt. Now put this over your head.' She handed him the black cotton sack she'd used to conceal the Glock. Once Baker had donned the sack, she signalled to Spooky, who got out of the Aurion and walked toward them holding a chemist bag.

Opening the driver's side door, he squatted on the ground and put the bag beside him. Grabbing Baker's right arm, he tightened his grip when the other man try to pull away. 'Don't worry, this won't hurt much.'

Removing a cufflink from Baker's shirt, he rolled the sleeve up past his elbow. Taking a tourniquet from the bag, he threaded it over Baker's arm and pulled it tight around his bicep.

'What's going on?' Baker's voice broke. 'What are you doing?'

'You'll be alright. Just stay still while I take some blood.'

'Blood? Why do you—' He bit back the words when Modeen once more prodded him with the Glock.

'Just settle down, Baker and you'll be alright.'

Spooky took a vacutainer from the bag and tore open its tightly-sealed sterile packaging. 'Now I want you to make a fist.' He swabbed Baker's arm with an alcohol wipe. 'Give that hand a couple of pumps for me ... that's it. Nice veins, by the way.' He threw Modeen a wink and then turned back to Baker. 'Now, you're going to feel a little sting.'

With practised skill he fingered the veins. Choosing one close to the surface that felt firm with blood, he inserted the needle. Baker's arm twitched as Spooky pressed a test tube into the vacutainer. When dark blood spurted into the tube, he reached up to release the tourniquet's pressure. 'It's a good hook-up. Haven't lost my touch.' He grinned at Modeen. 'What do you reckon, one vial or two?'

'Two. It needs to look convincing.'

Baker shook his head and gave a shuddering exhalation. 'What—'

'Hush, Baker,' she said soothingly, 'you're doing great. It's almost over.'

'Two it is.' Extracting the first full vial, Spooky inserted a fresh one. When it too was full he pulled the needle from Baker's arm and handed both warm tubes to Modeen. 'Tip 'em up and down to disperse the anticoagulant. That'll stop the blood from clotting.'

As Modeen obliged, Spooky wiped the spot of blood from the puncture in Baker's arm with another swab and then placed a Band-Aid over it. Rising to his feet he said, 'There you go, good as new. Now just one more thing. Put your head down and cup your face in your hands.'

When Baker hesitated, Spooky reached down and pushed his head toward his knees. Lifting the back of the cotton sack to expose Baker's scalp, Spooky grabbed a tuft of hair, whipped the knife out of his leg scabbard, and in one fluid motion sliced off a half inch square piece of scalp.

'Ahhh!' Baker bellowed and jerked upright, throwing up his hands. 'What the—'

Hastily passing the knife and piece of scalp to Modeen, Spooky grasped Baker's arms and forced them down. 'Sorry, mate, sorry. Take it easy. That's it, I'm not doing anything else. Now settle down so I can dress that wound.'

When Baker resisted, he cautioned, 'Don't forget there's a gun pointed at you.' He glanced at Modeen and pulled a face at her guilty grin and shrug.

She'd tucked the Glock into her waistband, needing both hands to juggle test tubes and knives while sealing the scalp tissue in a zip-lock plastic bag after first slicing it into smaller, jagged pieces.

But Baker wasn't to know that.

He sagged in the seat and Spooky released his arms to take an aerosol can of antiseptic from the chemist bag.

He sprayed the bleeding site of the excision and then dressed the wound. When he'd finished, he pulled the sack over the back of Baker's head again and wrapped a cotton bandage firmly around it.

Reaching around to clutch his head, Baker moaned, 'What are you *doing* to me? I don't understand ... please, tell me what's going on.'

Spooky patted his shoulder reassuringly. 'You'll be right, mate, don't worry. That's the worst over.'

Removing the rubber stoppers from the two test tubes, Modeen carefully poured the blood into the bag with the pieces of scalp, making sure not to spill any. When she zip-locked the bag and checked the seal was true, she nodded at Spooky.

He leaned across Baker and unclipped his seatbelt. 'Right, time to go.' Taking his arm, Spooky pulled him out and walked him to the rear of the Aurion. He clicked the remote and the boot popped open. Pausing to pat Baker down and check his pockets, he said, 'Hands behind your back.'

Baker exclaimed wearily, 'What now?' and reluctantly complied.

Spooky bound his hands with a thick cable tie and then pushed Baker's head down until he was bent double. 'In you go.' With firm hands, he folded Baker's five foot eleven frame into the compartment, doing his best to make the frightened man comfortable.

Inside Baker's government car, Modeen stuck the blood-filled plastic bag to the driver's side headrest with Band-Aids before walking around to stand in front of the vehicle. Lifting the Glock, she fired off one round. The bullet left a neat hole in the windscreen, but splattered the contents of the plastic bag inside the car. Going back to the driver's side, she pulled off the Band-Aid and plastic bag and was pleased to see a small entry hole in the headrest surrounded by blood, fragments of scalp tissue and hair. The bullet had blown apart the back of the headrest, leaving blood-splattered chunks of foam all over the back seat.

'Nice job.' Spooky strode up to join her. 'Baker's all tucked in so I'll cover our tracks, then we'll head to the apartment. Don't want to leave the poor buggar scrunched up in there too long.'

CHAPTER SEVEN

It was dusk when Wolf set off. He walked to the fence and scanned what he could see of the hundred acre farm that backed onto the houses along Crystal Brook Avenue. The farmland, stripped bare of trees, was all knee-high grass and lush rolling hills.

Feeling a light breeze blowing from the south, he decided to stick to the fence and come at the house from the north. As he straddled the barbed wire, he held up his phone and took a bearing on the location of TD93EM. Dropping to his belly, he crawled twenty metres into the farmland and then turned right and made his way parallel with the rear of the residential properties.

After crawling for a further hundred metres, he huddled low in the paddock grass and shielded his phone's screen to check the tracking app again. The green dot for TD93EM was seventy metres to his right.

He raised his head just enough to see over the waving tips of the grass.

The sun had set and the moon was barely casting a glow over the terrain, but he had a reasonable view from his elevated position. The house looked like a Tudor-styled domestic dwelling with two levels, three counting the garage at the base of the slope. Apart from a light in the lower level, there were no other signs of occupation.

His eyes were drawn to the rear of the house, where a yellow light lit up the back area beneath a patio. He saw the dark shape of a man sitting in a chair, cleaning something in his lap. Moments later the man lifted his arm toward the light and Wolf hastily ducked back down. While it was dark and he was seventy metres away, he recognised the distinctive silhouette of a pistol.

Well, I'm definitely in the right place.

Checking his app again, he concluded that the guard with the pistol was not TD93EM. By his reckoning, its location was on the northern side of the building a further ten metres to the left.

Securing his phone, Wolf crawled to the far corner of the house yard and tested the bottom barbed wire run of the fence with his hand. It had some give, so he slid underneath it and kept moving slowly and quietly on his belly in the grassy paddock next door. When he crawled into a thick pile of leaf litter about ten metres from the boundary fence, he decided it was a good spot to wait and watch. He wasn't there long before a light came on in the top storey attic window. Staring up at it, he could make out the horizontal bars across the opening.

To keep people out or in? he wondered.

There was sudden movement at the base of the house, and he crouched closer to the ground and froze as a guard came stomping around the corner with a dog in tow. When both guard and dog passed by the fence close to his location without hesitating, Wolf silently thanked the army for his training. He was downwind of them, so the dog hadn't picked up his scent.

When the muffled sound of a baby's cries reached his ears, he looked up and saw movement at the attic window. Moving stealthily, he pulled out his phone and used the camera function to zoom in on the window. When he saw a woman cradling a baby in her arms, Wolf felt a chill down his back.

TD93EM … EM ….

Emily.

Ben must've implanted his wife with a tracking device as a precaution.

Feeling anger and adrenaline building inside him, he clenched his teeth and resisted the impulse to charge the house and kick down the door. Forcing himself to stay calm, he retreated further into the paddock until sure he wouldn't be seen.

Pausing to take a couple of deep breaths, he rose to

his feet. Staying hunched over and keeping to the shadows just in case, he made a wide arc back to his vehicle.

———

Spooky pulled into the carpark in the basement of his building.

Modeen turned to him. 'Should we take the elevator or the stairs?'

'Normally I'd say the stairs, 'cos nobody uses them. But with old mate…' and he hitched his thumb toward the boot, '… being blindfolded, that's not gonna work.'

Modeen nodded. 'So it's the lift then?'

'Yeah. I'll go up and see if the coast is clear and unlock the apartment. Then I'll come back to hold the elevator and flag you in.'

'Roger.' Taking the car keys from him, Modeen got out, slipped into the driver's seat and reversed the car as close as she could get to the elevator. Then she went to the boot and waited. Five minutes later the elevator opened and Spooky stood holding the doors. He gave her a wave.

She took a quick look around the basement before popping the boot and grabbing Baker under the arm pits.

When she hauled him out of the boot, he staggered as his feet hit the ground. She steadied him and pulled him close with one arm as she closed the boot with her other hand. Walking him to the elevator, she pushed him inside and Spooky manoeuvred him so his back was against the rear wall. She pressed the remote to lock the car as Spooky held onto Baker and the lift doors closed.

Hitting the button for level eight, he murmured, 'So far so good.'

When the doors opened on their floor, they held their breath. Spooky stuck his head out and then gave Modeen a nod. They positioned themselves on either side of Baker and marched him straight into the apartment. Spooky kicked the door closed behind them and gestured to the spare bedroom. They guided Baker down the corridor and into the room, where they sat him on the bed.

Spooky cut the cable tie from Baker's hands and Modeen flicked him the car keys as he left the room.

Unwrapping the bandage, she removed the sack from Baker's head. She examined his wound and then re-fitted the bandage.

Baker blinked and muttered hoarsely, 'What's going on? Where am I?' He reached a tentative hand to finger the bandage, and felt around the back of his head gingerly.

She straightened to look down at him. 'You're going to stay here, out of sight, for the next few days.'

'What? No! I have a wife and children.' He jumped to his feet and made as if to push her aside, but gasped and winced when she intercepted his hand and brought him to his knees with a wrist lock.

Pulling the Glock out of the back of her pants, she placed the muzzle firmly in the centre of his forehead. 'We can do this the easy way or the hard way,' she said, keeping her voice even. 'I'll hog-tie you and leave you in the bottom of that wardrobe if I have to, or you can move about freely in this room and be relatively comfortable. The choice is yours.'

She used one knee to push him away and he fell back, cradling his wrist. He flicked her a miserable glance and then nodded his head in submission. Satisfied, she moved to check the window. Turning the key to the locked position, she removed it from the mechanism.

Next she checked the ensuite and the rest of the room for anything their detainee could use as a weapon, and then stopped at the door to gaze at the lock. With a significant glance at Baker, she pointed to the ensuite door. 'Go into the ensuite right now, and wait until I tell you to come out.'

He gave a disgruntled huff but did as she ordered.

She opened the bedroom door and called, 'You got a Phillips screw driver, Spook? We need to reverse this lock.'

He walked up holding a screwdriver and grinned at her. 'Great minds, Modeen.'

In a matter of minutes they had the lock reversed and Spooky left again.

Modeen knocked on the ensuite door. 'You can come out now, Baker.' When he appeared, she said pleasantly, 'Would you like a tea or coffee?'

'No.'

'Suit yourself. I'll bring you some dinner at seven-thirty.'

She walked out, locking the door behind her, and made her way to the kitchen where she placed the window key on the counter. Spooky was busy tinkering with his espresso machine.

'Up for a coffee?' he said, glancing over his shoulder at her.

'You bet.' She picked up her phone. 'Guess I'd better call it in.'

He nodded. 'Reckon we should alert the cops too. The sooner they find Baker's car, the sooner it'll be all over the news.'

Modeen tapped on Ben's number and didn't have to wait long for him to answer.

With an edge to his deep voice, he barked, 'Josephine, report.'

'Sir, the target has been neutralised, *sir*.'

There was a weighty pause on the other end of the phone, and this time when Ben spoke, his voice was calmer. 'Well done, Josephine.' With that, he ended the call.

Spooky had his phone out on the counter and dialled 000. A lady's voice answered. 'This is the emergency call centre. Do you require an ambulance, the fire brigade, or the police?'

'Police.'

'Please state your name, sir.'

'There's an abandoned white sedan behind the Devonport Street substation, near the Canberra nature park.'

'Sir, I need your name?'

'They're armed and a man's been shot.' He ended the call and handed Modeen a cup. 'There ya go, a flat white just how you like it. Now, I guess we just hurry up and wait … *again.*'

She frowned. 'I wish I knew what this was all about.' Taking the cup from him, she said, 'Well, Spook, I guess that's our part of the mission accomplished, for now.' She glanced at her watch. 'Bugs should be at the airport waiting for his flight to Kabul.'

Her phone vibrated with an incoming call and she snatched it up. 'Wolf, anything to report?'

'Yeah. I've checked out the Crystal Brook place in Porepunkah. There are two guards stationed outside the property, both armed. And … they have Emily and Chelsea. TD93EM is Emily Logan.'

CHAPTER EIGHT

'Hold on Wolf, I'll put you on speaker so Spooky can hear. We're in his apartment and have Harrison Baker secured and tucked away.' Modeen tapped on the speaker icon and placed her phone face-up on the counter. 'OK, go ahead.'

'TD93*EM*. The EM obviously stands for Emily. She and Chelsea are being held at the Porepunkah property.'

'*Ben's* Emily and Chelsea?' Spooky shook his head, looking stunned. 'Oh man … how many insurgents?'

'I only saw two sentries on duty outside, both armed. One was doing the rounds with a guard dog.'

Modeen nodded slowly. 'It's no wonder Ben hasn't been himself.'

'Yeah.' Spooky exhaled. 'No wonder.'

Closing her eyes in concentration as she put the pieces together Modeen said, 'This is all starting to make sense. Ben must be under close surveillance too. That's why he's working from home.' She opened her eyes again. '*And* why he couldn't tell us outright what was going on.'

'Well I'm all for tearing them a new one,' Wolf snarled. 'Holding a woman and a baby hostage … what a mongrel act.'

'Hold on. Let's keep our heads and go through what we know.' Hearing him exhale as though letting off steam, she went on. 'Firstly, I believe Emily and Chelsea were taken on Friday night – that's why Ben left early and why he looked like crap on Monday morning. It also explains why there are no event numbers for our missions, why he's been calling me "Josephine", and why we have additional tracking privileges. He's been dropping breadcrumbs, hoping we'd follow them.'

'Well, it worked,' Spooky said. 'Calling you "Josephine" certainly pressed your buttons.'

'Yeah.' She gave a wry grin. 'As he knew it would.'

'So they're using his family to force Ben to do their dirty work. To get rid of Baker and orchestrate Saddam Akim's release from prison.'

Wolf drawled, 'Saddam Akim?'

'He's a player in this big time,' Modeen said. 'I received an update from Bugs earlier on. His assignment is to collect Akim from a US military prison in Afghanistan and release him to the Spear of Allah.'

Wolf gave a long whistle and then announced,

'Right. So we go in and get Emily and Chelsea. Once they're out of danger the SoA won't have anything to bargain with, and Bugs can do what he likes with Akim. And you can probably guess what *I'd* like to do with him.'

Modeen raised questioning eyebrows at Spooky, and when he nodded his agreement she said, 'OK. As soon as Salty gets here, Spooky and I will head to Porepunkah. It's about a six hour drive so we should be there by o-three hundred. Wolf, is there anything in particular we need to bring?'

'Just the usual night viz gear, camo-webbing, and some comms wouldn't hurt either.'

Spooky murmured, 'Shouldn't be a problem.'

'OK. Sit tight Wolf, we'll be heading your way shortly.'

'I'm going back to keep them under surveillance. I'll meet you at the Crystal Brook Ave turn-off at o-three hundred.'

'Roger.' Modeen pressed End Call and got to her feet.

Spooky had just swallowed the last mouthful of coffee when his front door intercom buzzed. He pressed the answer button. 'Yeah?'

'Salty.'

'I'll be right down.'

Minutes later he returned with Salty in tow. The old man's long silver beard was neatly combed and he sported a black tee shirt and knee-length white cargo pants.

Modeen stepped forward to give him a hug. 'Nice to see you again, Salty.'

He gave her a squeeze and then held her at arms length. 'Say, weren't you blonde last time I saw you?'

Reaching up, she fingered the brunette wig. 'Why yes, I was.' She smiled. 'I mean … I am. I forgot I had this thing on.' Gripping the wig by the fringe, she pulled it off and flicked it onto the back of a kitchen stool. 'We're trying to stay incognito.' She rubbed both hands vigorously through her short blonde hair.

Salty nodded. 'I see.'

Behind them, Spooky collected the car keys and strode to the door. 'I'm going out to grab some pizza. Have you eaten, Salty?'

'Only airline food, youngster, so pizza sounds good to me. 'Specially one with plenty of anchovies.'

Spooky threw him a grin and said to Modeen, 'You bring Salty up to speed. As soon as I get back, you and I'll head.'

Nodding, she led Salty into the lounge room. As he took a seat she said, 'Can I get you a drink?'

'Nah, I got my caffeine top-up on the plane, thanks.'

'Right, well….'

When she'd finished recounting events, Salty sank back against the lounge chair. 'That gels with what I know.'

He glanced at Modeen. 'Ben contacted me outta the blue to ask if I had any contacts in Afghanistan, particularly in the US army. Told me he had to arrange for the release of a Saddam Akim into ASIO custody. He sounded plenty uptight, so I knew something big was goin' down. I got straight onto an old CIA buddy of mine, William Simpson, who called on his other mate, Mike Johnston. Together they were able to pull some strings to get Akim released for interrogation.'

Salty sat forward, clasping his hands together. 'Even then I suspected NatSec might not be totally *au fait* with what was goin' down.' He shook his head and after a long pause, looked at Modeen. 'So you want me to babysit this "Harrison Baker" bloke while you go off and rescue Ben's family?'

'That's pretty much it in a nutshell.' She regarded him levelly. 'Are you up for it?'

'Sure. Any chance I might get to shoot someone? Haven't had the pleasure in ages.' He gave her a cheesy smile and they both laughed.

'Sorry to disappoint you, but I'm hoping it doesn't come to that.' Chuckling at his fake hang-dog expression, Modeen got to her feet and pulled the wig back over her own hair. 'Anyway, come and I'll introduce you to your charge.' She led Salty into the spare bedroom.

Baker was sitting on the bed, leaning against the headboard with his head back and his eyes closed. Hearing them enter the room, he sat up straight and fixed Modeen with a doleful glare as she made the introductions.

'Harrison Baker, this is Salty. Salty, Harrison.' The two men studied each other assessingly as she continued. 'Salty will be looking after you for a while, so please try and behave yourself.'

'You people are in a lot of trouble,' Baker muttered belligerently.

Pulling the Glock from the back of her pants, she handed it to Salty. 'Baker knows the rules, Salty, so you shouldn't have to use this.'

'Aww...' Salty gave a mournful sigh, earning himself a worried frown from Baker.

'Maybe next time, old mate.' Modeen gave him a reassuring pat on the back as they turned and left the room.

She had discarded the wig once more and they'd settled themselves in the kitchen again when Spooky marched through the door and dropped a stack of pizzas on the counter, announcing cheerfully, 'What you don't eat, Salty, you can stick in the fridge and have later. There's milk in there too, and tea and coffee in the pantry. Make yourself at home. We're gonna eat on the fly.' Flipping the top pizza box off the stack, he nodded to Modeen.

Saying over her shoulder, 'We'll give you a call tomorrow, Salty,' she followed Spooky out the door.

'Have fun kids,' Salty called after them. 'And don't worry about me and Harrison, we'll be fine.'

.   .   .

With a squeal of tyres Spooky accelerated out of the basement carpark and headed over the Commonwealth Avenue Bridge across Lake Burley Griffin. Following their previous path around the Capital Hill ring road and onto Adelaide Avenue, they hit the Yarra Glen Highway.

Negotiating a roundabout at Wolden campus, he pulled off Athllon Drive into a block of self-storage units.

As he nosed the Aurion in between two rows of units and reversed the car up to a roller door, he said, 'There's a red remote control in the glove box.'

Modeen found the remote and pressed the button. When the roller door lifted, he reversed the car inside the unit. He tilted his head at the roller door and she pressed the button again to close it.

Getting out of the car, he switched on the lights in the unit. There was just enough room for Modeen to open her door and squeeze out. Making his way to the rear of the unit, he undid two huge padlocks on either side of another roller door and raised it to reveal an inner compartment.

Modeen breathed, 'Wow.'

The compartment only went back about a meter, but every bit of space was neatly stacked with shelves on one side and an assortment of rifles and hand guns on the other. Handing Modeen a Walther PPX, shoulder holster, silencer and two spare clips, Spooky clicked open the boot of the Aurion with his remote control.

She fluttered her eyelashes at him and said coyly, 'You shouldn't have,' at the same time adeptly pulling back the slide on the PPX and checking the breach.

'I've been saving that for just such an occasion.' He threw her a box of nine millimetre ammo.

She gave a regretful sigh. 'But I didn't get you anything.'

They both laughed and began loading the car's boot with gear. When they'd finished, Spooky stood at the boot and did a stocktake.

'Three comms units, three night vision head sets with thermal imaging, three MP5SD6s – including the one in the boot compartment – three pairs camouflage webbing and overalls, one Nemesis arms fifty cal Vanquish, and an M72LAW.'

Modeen raised a finger. 'I gave your Glock to Salty.'

'Ah.' Spinning on his heels, he picked up two Glock 17s, shoulder holsters, silencers, extra clips, and a leather harness containing two throwing knives.

She eyed the knives. 'I didn't know you could use them?'

He closed the boot with a thud. 'They're not for me, they're for the Wolfman. Right, let's make tracks.'

After driving the car out and carefully locking up both compartments of the unit, Spooky drove back onto Athllon Drive the way they'd come.

Modeen glanced at him. 'Shouldn't we be heading south?'

He grinned. 'I know it feels crazy, but it's definitely quicker if we take the Barton Highway up to Yass and then go down the Hume. Going south through Cooma on the Monaro Highway is more scenic, but with all the windy roads it'd put another hour on the trip.'

'Windy roads … I've had enough of them for a while.'

She threw him a rueful glance and they both chuckled at the reminder of her recent hair-raising chase down the winding Gillies Range in far north Queensland.

When her phone buzzed with an incoming call she looked at the caller ID, tapped on the answer icon, and placed the phone on speaker. 'You're on speaker phone, Bugs. I'm in a car with Spooky heading to Porepunkah.'

'Modeen, I've had further instructions from Ben. The US Army has transferred Akim from the main Parwan detention facility near Bagram, and I'm to collect him from Eggers Base as soon as my plane lands in Kabul. That's tomorrow, twenty hundred eastern standard time, thirteen hundred Kabul time. I'm to hand over Akim to some insurgents in a built-up residential area near the Khan Mosque. Right now, I'm about to get on the plane. What's the story with Porepunkah?'

'SoA is holding Emily and Chelsea hostage there.'

'They've got Ben's family?'

''Fraid so. Spooky and I are heading there now, to join Wolf.'

There was a pause and then Bugs said, 'Should I proceed as planned?'

'For now, yes. You have a stopover in Dubai, don't you?

'Yeah.' He swore under his breath. 'Five hours of coolin' my heels.'

'Call me from there. I should have an update for you by then.'

'How'd you get on with Baker?'

'Not a problem, Salty's looking after him. Hey, have you heard of a guy named Ivan Singh?'

'No, but Singh is a common name over there. It's like Smith, only times a thousand. What's his story?'

'He's the next ambassador in line after Baker.'

'Right. So possibly a player?'

'Possibly.'

'Well, take care in Porepunkah and watch your six.'

'Shall do. You too.'

———

Ben turned on the wide-screen television but didn't take a seat on the two-seater leather lounge chair he usually favoured. Instead, he remained standing, trying not to look at the hollowed-out place on the chair where his wife would normally sit snuggled against his broad frame, or down at the floor where his baby daughter often lay on a bunny rug kicking her chubby legs and gurgling up at him.

Steeling himself, he flicked agitatedly through the channels until he hit the evening news. After watching for a few seconds, he shouted to Khalil, 'Tell your boss to turn on the news, *now*.'

Picking up his mobile, Khalil tapped in a number and placed it to his ear. 'He wants you to look at the news on the TV, urgently.' He kept the phone against his ear as the main news story unfolded on the screen.

Ben turned up the volume as a shapely, twenty-something news reporter spoke into the camera. 'Mystery surrounds the disappearance of The Honourable Harrison Baker, who was due to replace Andre Kane, the current Australian Ambassador to Afghanistan. Mr Baker's car was found abandoned at this power substation.'

With a sweep of her arm, she indicated the backdrop behind her where police officers could be seen milling around Baker's government car. 'Authorities hold grave fears for the Ambassador's safety.'

The camera panned to the car and zoomed in on the bullet hole in the windscreen. There was a brief glimpse of the mangled, blood-spattered driver's headrest inside, before the reporter stepped back into the frame.

'Stay tuned for more details in our main story tonight.'

Khalil listened for a moment and then walked over to shove his mobile in Ben's face. Jerking his chin, he indicated for Ben to take the phone.

When he put it to his ear, Ben heard a smug Australian voice say, 'Good work, I see you're cooperating, Ben. Keep it that way and you'll get your family back unharmed.'

'I've done as you asked,' Ben barked. 'Arrangements have been made for Akim's release. So let my family go, Gator.'

'Oh, but I *like* giving you orders and having you take them!' His tone was mocking. 'I want to make the most of it while I can.' Suddenly serious, he snarled, 'When, and *only* when, we are certain Akim is safely with us will you get your family back.' There was a click and then silence.

Ben's eyes glittered menacingly as he lowered the phone and dropped it into Khalil's waiting hand.

CHAPTER NINE

Turning off the Barton Highway at Yass, Spooky and Modeen headed down the Hume toward Gundagai. It was twenty-three fifteen and they'd been on the road for just over two and a half hours.

Bored, Modeen filled some of the time by loading cartridges into the spare clips of the Walther PPX and the MP5s.

She glanced at Spooky. 'You got any clips that need filling?'

Keeping his eyes on the road, he reached into a top pocket and pulled out four spare clips for his Glock 17s and handed them to her. 'Nine millimetre parabellums, please.' When she blew him a raspberry, he gave a bemused grin. 'What?'

'*Parabellums?*' She sniggered. 'Oh please. You're not Jack Reacher.'

He chuckled. 'What d'ya mean? That's what the DWM manufacturers in Germany call them.'

'Exactly, and you know why?'

''Cos it sounds cool?'

She rolled her eyes. 'Parabellum is derived from the Latin *si vis pacem, para bellum,* which translated means "if you seek peace, prepare for war". But the DWM could've just as easily called them something else, like ... "roosters".'

He gave a bark of laughter. 'Fine. Please fill my clips with nine millimetre roosters.'

She chuckled, 'One clip of roosters coming right up.'

Their laughter subsided until the only sound in the cabin was road noise, and the snap of bullets into clips as Modeen filled them.

Spooky flicked her a sideways glance before returning his gaze to the road ahead. 'So you and Wolf ... how long has that been going on?'

She stiffened and eyed him warily before mumbling, 'Since not long after I started at NatSec.'

'How serious is it?' He stared straight ahead as though knowing he was treading a dangerous path.

'About as serious as two agents can ever be.' She frowned. ''Specially when they live on opposite sides of Australia.'

'Yeah, that's gotta be tough.' He risked a quick glance at her. 'I'm happy for both of you, but I have to admit it took me by surprise, considering all the effort we went to in the special forces to overlook the whole gender thing.'

'Yeah, but that was then and this is now.' Gazing out the window, she mused aloud, 'It was a condition of my appointment to the SASR that my unit be able to see me as a soldier, not as a woman, in all situations.' She turned to look at him. 'And you guys did it. I'll always be grateful to you for that.'

'Speaking for myself, and probably the other blokes as well, we regarded ourselves as soldiers first, men second. We simply applied that to you as well after you'd won our respect, which any new team member, male or female, had to do.'

'Yes we bonded well as a team.' She looked away again, pressing her lips together. 'And we knew losing friends was an occupational risk when we signed up.'

There was a weighty pause and then he said quietly, 'You thinking about Gator too?'

'Mmm.' She gave a slow nod. 'I feel guilty but ... I can't help thinking that while PTSD might be making him act out of character, that doesn't change the fact that he's betrayed our trust and his country.'

Glancing across at Spooky, she said gravely, 'But that same bloke saved us on numerous occasions in action.' She shook her head. 'It's such a shame that he couldn't get the right help when he needed it. I hope he doesn't put us in the situation where we have to....' She blinked and swallowed.

'Don't forget we saved him plenty of times too.

Look, Gator and I were probably closer than anyone in our unit, and I understand that it's not his fault he's suffering from PTSD. But when it comes down to it, for whatever reason, he's chosen his side. And he has to accept the outcomes of his choices, just like we do.'

Modeen regarded him levelly for a long moment before giving a solemn nod.

———

Salty opened the bedroom door carrying two pizza boxes. 'You've got a choice, Harrison. Supreme or meat lovers.'

The bedroom was empty but the light was on in the ensuite. Hearing the toilet flush, Salty bent to put the pizzas on the foot of the bed. He flipped opened the lids and breathed in the rich, aromatic steam that wafted out. Behind him, the door to the ensuite opened quietly.

Seeing Salty with his back to him, Baker seized the opportunity and sprang forward to throw an arm around Salty's neck. At just over five foot eleven he was a good two inches taller, at least thirty kilos heavier, and thirty years younger.

He yelled triumphantly, 'I've got you now, old man.'

The sudden pressure on his neck had Salty gagging and clutching at Baker's arm, until he shifted his body to the left and dropped his right hand. Making a fist, he brought it forward and then hammered it sharply back into his captor's groin.

When Baker gasped and reeled forward in pain, Salty flicked his head up and back, clocking Baker soundly under the chin.

His head jerked and he staggered back and hit the wall. As he rebounded toward Salty, the old man grabbed his arm and used his forward momentum to throw him onto the bed.

After he'd stopped bouncing, Baker shook his head and groaned. Rolling over and pushing himself up on his arms, he shuffled back up the bed to slump against the headboard, glaring accusingly at Salty and rubbing his jaw. When he felt wetness, he looked at his fingers and saw blood. Grimacing, he felt around his mouth and found a split top lip.

Salty said cheerfully, 'So Harrison, was that supreme or meat lovers? While you're choosing, I'll go get some tissues for that lip. You know, you really should be more careful.' He disappeared from the room and returned with a box of tissues, which he threw on the bed in front of Baker.

'My family's going to be worried sick,' Baker muttered, his swelling lip starting to affect his speech. Tearing a tissue from the box, he dabbed his mouth. 'What's this all about anyhow? Why are you people holding me here? And what's with the teddy bear torture?' He fingered the peeling Band-Aid on the venepuncture site on his arm, and the cleanly-dressed wound on the back of his head.

Salty perched himself at the end of the bed, near the pizza boxes. 'Look, you might not believe this, but these people are trying to help. Your name came up, and you're lucky they got to you first. Otherwise your family would've found you at the bottom of Lake Burley Griffin wearing cement shoes.'

'My name came up on what?'

'On the wrong people's list.'

'Oh, for—' Baker exhaled sharply. 'Look, if you're on my side then why don't you let me call my family and tell them I'm alright? Just one phone call, that's all I'm asking for.'

'Now think about it, Harrison. I doubt you'd want your loved ones mixed up in this. There's safety in ignorance.' Salty pulled off another bit of pizza and took a bite.

'Mixed up in what? I don't even know *that!* Or how long you're going to hold me.' Baker threw down the bloody tissue he'd had against his lip and ripped another one from the box.

'As long as it takes. Don't worry, we'll have you back before you know it.' Salty paused. 'Say, do you want a beer?'

Baker pressed the tissue against his lip and looked at Salty as though he were crazy. 'No, I don't want a *beer.*'

'Suit yourself, youngster. Always reckon pizza

tastes better with beer.' Salty shared the remaining slices between the two boxes and got to his feet. Lifting one of the boxes, he shrugged at Baker. 'Sing out if you change your mind.'

Ambling out of the room, he locked the door behind him.

———

The Aurion's headlights lit up the road sign.

'Gundagai,' Spooky announced. 'Good, we'll pull in and fill up. Should only be a bit over three hours to Porepunkah from here.'

Slowing the car, he drove into a twenty-four hour service station and parked beside a petrol bowser. While filling the car with unleaded fuel, he bent level with the driver's side window to ask a yawning Modeen, 'Want anything from the shop?'

'No, I'm fine thanks Spook.'

'Wanna drive for a bit? I wouldn't mind a break from the white line fever.'

She sat forward. 'Sure, it'll help me stay focused.'

'Right, jump behind the wheel. I'll go and settle the bill.'

Taking her phone from her pocket, Modeen got out and went around to the driver's side. Leaning against the warm car, she sent Wolf a text.

ETA 3 hours.

By the time Spooky came back, she was behind the

wheel with the motor running. As soon as he was seated, she nosed the Aurion out of the service station and accelerated back onto the Hume Highway.

Spooky sighed and reclined his seat. Opening the can of Coke he'd bought from the servo, he took a mouthful and mused aloud, 'What d'ya reckon the chances are of Gator being at the Porepunkah place?' He looked at Modeen. 'What's your radar telling you?'

She took her time answering. 'Well, we know the SoA is desperate to get Saddam Akim released from prison. We also know that Gator was one of the major players in their last attempt during the G20 summit.'

They shared a significant glance as she continued. 'The fact they've now kidnapped Ben's family and are blackmailing him tells me that Gator is definitely involved. In fact, I wouldn't be surprised if he were leading the operation.'

He frowned. 'You really think so?'

'Think about it, Spook. We know Gator had issues with authority even back in the SASR, so apart from the whole SoA thing I think this is his way of getting back at Ben.'

'But why Ben? Gator would've had other COs during his time in the force.'

'Well, for one thing, Ben didn't support his application for promotion. And for another thing, his size, commanding demeanour and of course his VC, makes Ben a very obvious authority figure.'

'Oh yeah.' Spooky gave a snort. 'I remember Gator

tackling Ben about not supporting his application. For a while I thought it might come to blows, but he's smart enough to know that'd be a losing gambit.'

'And that also means Gator will be careful.' Her eyes narrowed. 'If I were stupid enough to take Ben's family hostage I'd want to keep them close, *very* close. So yes, I think Gator will be at the property, or not far away.'

Spooky nodded gravely. 'Well, I guess we'll find out soon enough.'

CHAPTER TEN

I t was just past o-three hundred. Modeen reached across to touch Spooky on the forearm. He sat up, blinking.

'We're on Mount Buffalo Road, Spook. Crystal Brook Ave should be coming up shortly on the left.'

'Wooh….' He yawned, stretched, and arched his back. 'Man, that was a great little power nap. I don't even remember closing my eyes.' He rubbed his face with both hands and sniffed. Looking up, he stiffened and pointed to the right side of the road ahead. 'Hey, look.'

Peering into the dimness, Modeen saw the glow of a faint light. Slowing the vehicle, she pulled in alongside it. Wolf slipped his mobile into his pocket and jumped into the back seat behind her.

'Turn right here, then take that side track on the left just before the bridge.'

She followed his directions and parked in a hidden clearing parallel to Mount Buffalo Road.

Turning off the motor, she swivelled in her seat to look at Wolf. 'What's the situation?'

'The house is a two storey Tudor-style residence. It's in darkness except for the kitchen at the rear. Three guards and one dog outside, three guards inside. The guards swap shifts every four hours. They're due to change again in an hour's time. Emily and Chelsea are being held on the top floor on the northern side. If we saddle-up here and cross the main road, we can head upwind to the boundary fence below her window.'

At Modeen's brisk nod, Spooky said firmly, 'Right, let's do this.'

All three got out of the Aurion to huddle around the boot, where Spooky distributed the camouflage overalls, webbing, and night vision goggles. They'd finished putting on the overalls when Spooky handed Wolf a shoulder holster containing a Glock 17 fitted with a silencer, and two spare clips.

'Oh yeah, and I brought this for you too.' He passed Wolf the throwing knives and harness.

Taking out one of the knives, Wolf eyed it critically. Hardened stainless steel in gun-barrel black, it was nine inches long.

He balanced it in his hand and then pushed it back into the scabbard. 'Nice.' When he slid the harness across his shoulders, it positioned the knives flat against the centre of his back at shoulder blade height.

Watching him, Modeen asked, 'What's the layout of the house?'

He donned his night vision goggles and looked down at the ground. Brushing away the roadside gravel with a boot, he cleared a space in the dirt. Then he grabbed a small stick and broke it in half. When he squatted and began drawing in the dirt, the other two slipped on their goggles and moved in close.

Sketching a rough square he muttered, 'This is the house. Front door on the left, eastern side,' and he made smaller scratches in the dusty soil, 'and back door on the west. We'll be coming at them from the north.' He drew an arrow pointing toward the house representing their approach.

'Emily and Chelsea are on the top floor here.' Poking the stick into the dirt, he made a small mark. 'There are bars across the inside of their dormer window. There's one guard at the front.' Making more dots with the stick's tip, he indicated the guards' locations. 'One at the back, and the third with the dog circles the perimeter. He's carrying a carbine and wearing night vision goggles, the others all have automatic pistols.' Dropping the stick, he rose to his full height.

As they shrugged into their shoulder holsters and webbing, Modeen handed them each a comms earpiece. 'Is there any way of getting up to Emily's window from the outside?'

Wolf nodded. 'There's a fairly sturdy-looking pergola covered in a climbing plant just beneath it.'

Picking up the stick, Modeen knelt on one knee by the dirt diagram. In a low but commanding voice she said, 'OK. Like Wolf said, we'll come at the house from the north. We'll hold up here,' and she put a cross on the northern side of the square, 'and take out the guard with the dog when they circle close. Spook, I want you at Emily's window, ready to go. Wolf, you take out the front guard to the east, and I'll take out the rear guard on the western side. Once they're down we'll move inside on my signal.' The two men nodded their understanding as Modeen tossed the stick into the grass and straightened, scuffing her foot over the diagram.

Picking up an MP5SD6, Wolf inserted a thirty round magazine into its base, palmed it home and pushed the safety lever forward. Pulling back the slide, he released it, loading the first bullet into the chamber as the others followed suit. Growling, 'Follow me,' he disappeared into the gloom.

———

Ben sat up in bed, eyes fixed on his phone and its tracking app. He held his breath and watched as three green dots converged near the Noonameena Bridge next to Crystal Brook Avenue in Porepunkah. As the dots crossed Mount Buffalo Road and made their way slowly toward the fourth green dot of TD93EM, he sprang to his feet and, carefully tucking his mobile out of sight, made his way downstairs.

Passing Omar curled up on the sofa asleep, he continued into the kitchen, where Khalil whirled around from watching the wall-mounted TV to eye him warily. He smirked. 'You still having trouble with the sleeping?'

Ben said nothing as he picked up the kettle, filled it with water at the sink, and plugged it in. Taking a mug from the cupboard above the kettle, he loaded it with a heaped teaspoon of instant coffee and one of sugar.

Khalil watched him closely at first but got bored and turned his attention back to the sleazy B-grade movie playing on the TV.

Pulling up a chair on the opposite side of the island bench to Khalil, Ben slid his mobile onto his lap so he only had to flick his eyes downward to see it, and sat waiting for the kettle to boil.

———

Wolf led them across the first property. It was peppered with fir and ash trees and had a cleared area in its centre large enough for a future shed or house.

The ground was damp with dew and the early morning still held only a hint of moonlight. Their night vision goggles gave the landscape a green hue and made their cross-country trek easy.

At Wolf's signal, they slung their rifles onto their backs and got down on their bellies to crawl in single file across the next property. Its terrain was more heavily wooded, with groves of fir and ash trees spaced closer together with thick piles of leaf litter beneath them.

At approximately seventy metres from the house, Wolf gave another signal and moved to his left. Modeen and then Spooky came up on his right until all three were spaced out in a line. Using a thick clump of leaf litter as cover, they unslung their rifles and scanned the yard between them and the house.

Modeen switched her goggles to thermal imaging and whispered, 'No heat signatures.'

'Guard at ten o'clock,' Spooky hissed.

Switching her goggles back to night vision, she watched as a Doberman appeared around the corner to her left, towing a guard. After negotiating a path between trees and around garden beds, the guard headed in a direction that would take him parallel to and twenty metres in front of the three concealed agents.

Easing the safety lever slowly back one notch on his MP5 to place it into single shot mode, Wolf pushed the muzzle of the weapon through the leaf litter. 'I'll take the guard.'

Spooky murmured, 'I've got the dog.'

The guard made slow progress behind the dog which moved from side to side, straining at the end of the leash, its eager nose never more than a few inches from the ground.

When dog and guard were in front of the three agents, Spooky inched back the safety lever on his rifle. At the faint click, the dog's head flew up and it froze, legs splayed stiffly in front of it. Pricking its ears, it sniffed the air.

Spooky whispered, 'In three … two … one.'

At almost the same instant he and Wolf let loose a single round.

A low-pitched hiss erupted from their weapons and twenty metres away, the guard and dog dropped to the ground and lay still. Pausing briefly to listen for any reaction, the three agents crawled forward and slipped under the bottom rung of the wire fence.

Thankfully, it wasn't barbed wire so they slid through easily enough. On the other side of the fence they got to their feet and, keeping low and quiet, swiftly covered the remaining forty metres to the pergola beneath Emily's window.

Wolf arrived first and put his back to a solid six-by-six inch corner post. As he dropped to one knee and put his hands palms-up on the other, Modeen stopped short to provide cover.

Slinging his rifle, Spooky moved up and put his left foot into Wolf's hands and his right foot onto Wolf's left shoulder. Wolf straightened to his full height and gave Spooky an upward boost. He landed smoothly with very little noise on top of the pergola.

Balancing on one of the beams like a tightrope walker, Spooky made his way to the tiled roof of the house. Creeping up to the dormer window, he ran his hand across the pane and pulled the bayonet from his ankle strap.

The weather-worn frames offered little resistance when he stealthily prised the windows open. He felt the bars.

Hmm … firm but not too firm.

On a small table just inside the window he could see a bag whose butterfly and elephant pattern said 'baby' loud and clear. Looking further in, he saw a sleeping form in the double bed he could easily imagine was Emily with Chelsea by her side.

Moving back down to where the pergola met the roof, he whispered, 'Spook ready.'

Wolf crept around to the eastern side of the building with his MP5 at the ready. Keeping low, he skirted the garden. Seeing a guard sitting on a brick planter box beside the cobblestone path leading from the front door to the driveway, Wolf crept up behind him. Pressing his rifle's muzzle against the base of the man's skull, he pulled the trigger.

As the guard slumped forward, Wolf grabbed him by the back of his collar and lowered him to the path.

Picking up the guard's nine millimetre Sig, he dropped it underneath the thick foliage in the planter box and whispered into his comms set, 'Wolf ready.'

Modeen made her way to the western side of the building and saw a guard sitting on the back patio.

The area was partly enclosed with lattice and its roof dripped with grape and passionfruit vines. The guard's silhouette was clearly visible against the yellowish light streaming from the kitchen window. He sat dozily cradling a pistol in his lap, his fat belly propping him back in his seat.

Slinging her MP5, Modeen pulled the Walther PPX from her shoulder holster. Carefully pushing the pistol's silencer through the lattice, she let loose one round. The guard slumped forward and a tiny spot of blood dribbled from a hole in the temple of his melon-like head.

CHAPTER ELEVEN

Sitting at the island bench, Ben raised his cup and drained the last mouthful of coffee that by now was luke-warm.

Khalil was just finishing a phone check-in with his boss.

Taking a quick look down at his mobile, Ben held his breath as his eyes sought the three green dots on the tracking app that were Modeen, Wolf and Spooky. He found them, mere metres from Emily's location and closing in. Breathing out, he slipped the mobile into a pants pocket and got up to drop his coffee mug into the sink. About to walk past Khalil, he paused.

Ready with a sneer, Khalil glanced up at him in time to see Ben's hands snake out and clamp his head in a vice-like grip, one hand over his mouth the other on the back of his head.

Panic flooded into Khalil's eyes, but before he could react Ben reefed his head sideways, snapping his neck. When his body went limp, Ben lowered it to the floor. Taking out the tracking device Catalina had planted in his phone case, he bent and slipped it into Khalil's top pocket.

Straightening, he peered into the lounge room. Seeing no movement, he made his way quietly into the room until he was standing over Omar, who was still fast asleep on the sofa.

Staring down at him, Ben noted the awkward angle of the guard's head where it was propped on top of the armrest. His body was chest-down on the sofa's seat and his left leg dangled off the end.

Lifting his right foot and aiming at the base of Omar's neck, Ben made a downward thrust with all his weight behind it. Omar's head snapped back sickeningly against Ben's lower leg as his shoulders and chest were pushed through the collapsing sofa.

Staring down at the dead man, Ben gave a grunt. Turning on his heels, he strode back through the kitchen, rapping out orders on his mobile on the way.

———

'On my mark,' Modeen whispered into the comms. She stepped into the light on the back patio.

The fat guard was still in his chair, chin on his chest, not moving. The front of his shirt, stretched tight over his bulging stomach, was dark with blood. She peered through the kitchen window and hissed, 'Wait.'

Inside, a guard sat alone at the kitchen table. He held a tumbler of what looked like a short black espresso, and had a Browning nine millimetre pistol on the table in front of him.

Easing her PPX through a gap in the open casement window, Modeen pressed the end of the silencer against the insect screen and waited until the guy had put down the tumbler. When he obliged a moment later, she squeezed the trigger and he sagged forward, his head landing on the table with a dull thud.

Moving to the back door, she tried the knob. It was locked. She took three steps back and once more whispered, 'On my mark.'

Feeling the adrenalin building inside her, she transferred her weight onto her back foot and lunged at the door, yelling, 'Go!'

As she kicked the door in, on the roof above Spooky leapt from the edge and dove through the open dormer window holding his MP5 close.

The security bars gave way under his weight, and on landing he executed a smooth forward roll.

Emily awoke with a scream and reached for Chelsea, clutching her murmuring baby close to her chest.

Springing to his feet Spooky whispered, 'Don't worry, Emily. It's me, Luke.'

She peered into the darkness trying to see, and stuttered, 'L-luke?'

'Yes, shhh! And stay low.' He pushed the double bed ensemble closer to the wall and lifted the end, causing Emily to slide to the floor, still holding Chelsea. Flipping it over, he rested the end of the bed against the wall, effectively encasing the hostages in a padded triangular cell.

Spinning around, he levelled his MP5 at the door.

And waited.

Downstairs, Wolf had taken three long strides and kicked in the front door, exploding it off its hinges. But as he stepped into the small front foyer he was grabbed and slammed against the wall to his left.

Before he could recover, he was picked up and slammed against the wall to his right. He tried to pull his Glock from its holster but before he could get it clear, two gigantic fists pounded his chest and threw him against the opposite wall.

As he struggled with his powerful opponent, he heard his Glock hit the floor with a metallic thump.

Checking the kitchen on her way in, Modeen eyed the guard slumped over the table. He hadn't moved and there was a bloody hole to the right side of his forehead.

She kept moving toward the main living area where a light had been flicked on. Entering the room cautiously, she saw Gator standing in its centre, aiming a pistol at the front entrance.

Gator.

So it's really true.

Leaping forward, she kicked the pistol out of his hand.

He staggered back, bellowing, 'Kill the hostages!' to a sentry standing at the top of the stairs.

Shouting, 'No!' Modeen raised her Walther toward the guard but before she could fire Gator yanked her backward by the hair.

Tugging a bayonet from his leg strap, he pulled her close against him and pressed the blade to her throat.

Above them, the guard on the landing disappeared into a room and two shots rang out.

'You're too late,' Gator sneered in her ear. 'Drop your weapon or I'll slit your throat.'

She let her pistol slip from her fingers and watched helplessly as a giant of a man dragged Wolf into the room and lifted him by the throat to hold him against the wall. Modeen couldn't help a tiny whimper at the sight of Wolf's legs searching desperately for the ground, his head looking small above the man's massive hands.

Tilting back his head, the giant gave a belly laugh. Wolf's face contorted as he arched his back and thrust his head forward, at the same time throwing his arms up and back. He grasped the two knives in the harness at his back and ripped them from their scabbards.

The giant's laughter stopped abruptly and his eyes widened as Wolf raised his arms above his head, reversed the knives in his hands, and brought them down hard, plunging the blades into either side of the man's neck. With a startled grunt, the man fell backward as Wolf dropped to the floor, gasping for air.

'Impressive, Wolf,' Gator muttered darkly. 'They still call you that don't they?'

Recovering quickly, Wolf moved closer and fixed his old army buddy with steely eyes. 'Let her go, Gator,' he growled.

'You're not in any position to give me orders. And I'm *sick* of being ordered around, I've had enough of that, 'specially from *VC Ben Logan*.' Gator spat the words, and pressed the blade firmer against Modeen's throat, making her gasp and wince. 'Drop the knives, Wolf, or you'll be the last thing she sees.'

Glimpsing a manic glint in Gator's eyes, Wolf froze. He dropped the knives to the floor at his feet and stood unarmed with his hands palms forward and loose at his sides. With a shake of his dark head he muttered, 'What happened to you, man?'

Gator glared at him. 'I got smart.'

Ignoring him, Wolf said, 'That's Modeen you've got there. *Modeen.*'

'You think I'm an idiot?' Gator rasped. 'I know who it is.'

'Then you know you don't want to hurt a member of our team.'

'Team?' Gator scowled and his face twisted. 'Oh we were a team alright, *once,* when it suited you all. And when it didn't, you just went your separate ways.'

His voice rose and his complexion darkened. 'Where were you all when I needed you most? You have no idea what I was going through, what—' He bit back the last words when he saw Wolf take a step forward.

Roaring, 'Stop where you are!' he took an unsteady breath and tightened his grip on Modeen.

Wolf grew still and fixed his eyes on hers.

Gator released some of the pressure on the blade but kept it close against her skin. Staring hard at Wolf, he said incredulously, 'What? You two?' He pulled Modeen tighter against himself and sneered, 'I thought you had better taste than that, girl.' His eyes narrowed. 'Now, is it just a cosy twosome we have here or are there more of you? Where's the sneaky little one? Where's Spooky?'

'Right here,' a voice called from the top landing.

With a jolt, Gator turned to look up at the voice just as Spooky squeezed the trigger on his Glock. As Gator's head rocked sideways, Modeen grabbed his knife arm and held it away from her throat while his body collapsed, sliding to the floor. In the silence that followed, Wolf hurried to Modeen's side to check she was alright, and then the three of them bowed their heads and stared at the lifeless body of their old army mate.

Squatting beside him, Modeen put a gentle hand to the side of Gator's face and then glanced up at Spooky on the landing. 'Emily?'

'In here, safe.' Spooky went back into the bedroom. Turning on the light, he went to the ensemble leaning against the wall and grasped it by the top. Behind him, Modeen had run up the stairs and entered the room, stepping over the body of the guard.

She watched Spooky pull the ensemble off the wall to reveal Emily huddled in the corner holding Chelsea.

Hurrying to her side, Modeen said gently, 'You're safe now, Em.' She extended a hand and helped Emily to her feet. Opening her mouth to speak, Emily instead burst into tears. Modeen put an arm around her shaking shoulders as Emily looked over at Spooky. Gesturing for him to come closer, she put a trembling hand on his arm and sobbed, 'Thank you.'

Standing in the doorway, Wolf said gruffly, 'I guess we're right to contact Ben now. I'll call it in.'

Modeen gave him a nod and he went back downstairs. Taking out his phone, he dialled Ben's number. His call was answered before the first ring had finished chiming.

'Report!' Amid a lot of background noise, Ben's voice was thick with tension.

Wolf rapped, 'They're both safe.'

'Say again!' Ben barked anxiously.

Raising his voice to compensate for the noise, Wolf said, 'They're both safe, Ben. Emily and Chelsea are safe.'

He heard the whoosh of Ben's deep exhalation against the speaker, and could imagine his expression of profound relief.

After a pause, Ben said, 'And our team?'

'All good.'

'Well done.' Ben sighed again. 'I'm just boarding a Blackhawk. Will be there in fifty minutes.'

'We'll need some cleaners here.' Wolf began walking toward the staircase.

'I'll send them up there after they've finished at my house.' Ben paused. 'Gator?' His tone was low, apprehensive.

Wolf took a breath and said in a gravelly voice, 'He didn't give us a choice.' Climbing the stairs, he strode into the bedroom, saying, 'There's someone here who I'm pretty sure will want to talk to you. I'll hand you over now,' and he passed the phone to a teary Emily.

The three agents left to give her some privacy. On their way out of the room, Wolf grabbed the body of the guard on the floor by the collar of his shirt and dragged him out. 'Ben's on his way,' he puffed to the other two. 'He'll be here in about fifty minutes.'

Spooky thumped him on his broad back. 'I guess we'd better clean up then.'

'Nah, Ben's sending the cleaners. But I reckon we should at least stack the bodies out of the way.' Pausing, Wolf looked thoughtful and said drily, 'We're gonna need a crane for the big bloke in the front foyer.' After he'd hauled the body into the back room, he emerged to find Spooky standing gazing down at Gator.

Going to his side, he put a hand on Spooky's shoulder. 'You did the right thing, mate. It was either him or the two of us.'

'Why,' Spooky mumbled, 'after all we've been through as a team? What makes a person go from being a team player to *this?*' He shook his head sadly. 'Looking down at him from up there, I *knew* it was Gator but it also wasn't him, if that makes any sense. He seemed so *different*, almost like a stranger.'

'He wasn't the Gator we knew, Spook, and you can blame the PTSD for that. Some people can work through it, some can't, and I guess it comes down to how you manage the condition. Maybe Gator was just too high strung. He was a creative soldier and brilliant with explosives—' Wolf clicked his fingers. 'That reminds me, we'd better check this place thoroughly, just in case.' Spotting a laptop and audio equipment in the corner of the room, he strode over to it. 'Well,' he drawled, tapping on the keyboard and eyeing the screen, 'I guess this is how they were keeping Ben in check.'

———

A Blackhawk helicopter thundered low over Crystal Brook Avenue, scouting for a level landing site. When minutes later it touched down in the farmland at the back of the property, Ben leapt out and ran to the front entrance of the Porepunkah house. The ruined front door had been picked up from off the floor and now leaned against the wall to the left of the foyer. Striding past it, Ben saw Emily racing down the corridor toward him holding up the skirt of her red evening dress so she wouldn't trip over it.

Sobbing, she cried, 'Ben!' and sprang into his open arms.

He lifted her off her feet, holding her close against him, his lips pressed against her face. His own face was unshaven and it was obvious he hadn't had much sleep, but he stood tall with a new vitality to his six foot four frame now his wife was safely back in his arms.

Modeen stood behind them, cradling a gurgling Chelsea.

Seeing her, Ben lowered Emily and choked, 'Chels.'

When he reached out an arm for his baby daughter, Modeen stepped closer to pass her to him, only to find herself pulled in tight. He dropped a kiss on her forehead as Emily too hugged her warmly.

'Thanks JD, you're one of a kind. I knew you and

the team would work it out.' Ben's voice was deep and gravelly with emotion.

Releasing her, he took Chelsea and lifted her above his head. While Emily looked on, smiling through grateful tears, the little girl chuckled and waved her chubby hands at him, clearly delighted to see her daddy. When he lowered Chelsea again to cradle her in his strong arms, he glanced at Modeen. 'Spook and Wolf?'

'In the back room.' She inclined her head down the corridor.

He nodded and handed Chelsea to Emily. 'We're leaving in fifteen minutes, Em.' He kissed her again and stroked the baby's head before making his way to the study.

When he entered the back room, he found Wolf and Spooky standing over Gator. They had separated his body from the others and covered it with a crocheted rug from the lounge.

Ben looked at them and then squatted beside the body. Pulling back the rug, he stared at Gator's face for a long moment. When Modeen joined them, he pulled the rug back up and rose to his full height. Taking a deep breath, he eyed each of them individually.

'Have you guys come to terms with this? Are we good?' When he received tentative nods in reply, he said, 'I'll make sure he receives the usual military burial for a soldier KIA. His ex-wife and family don't need to know about this,' and he indicated the mayhem around them with a sweep of a muscular arm. 'We owe him that much for his honourable actions in the past.'

The other three nodded gravely and after a minute Wolf said, 'So, what now?'

Ben's mouth set in a grim line. 'Now we end this.'

CHAPTER TWELVE

Ben settled a more composed Emily under the picture window in the lounge room and handed her Chelsea. Murmuring, 'Won't be long, Hon,' he dropped a kiss on the top of Emily's head before joining his agents at the dining room table.

As he took a seat, Modeen leaned in and said in a low voice, 'I've asked Bugs to put a tracker on Akim so we'll know where to find him.'

Ben nodded. 'Excellent. With a bit of luck he'll lead us to his associates, and best case scenario, he'll lead us to their nest. Which brings me to Bugs. He's going to need a hand.'

'He's got an army mate he reckons is trustworthy and can handle himself,' Modeen informed him. 'He'll be with Bugs for the transfer.'

'Good.' Ben gave another approving nod. 'From all indications, the funds for the SoA's operations have been flowing into an account held by Akeem Jibril in Kabul. I think it's safe to assume their operation's based there.'

He glanced around the table making eye contact with each of them in turn. 'After what they've shown themselves capable of, I want to make sure we shut down as many of their operations as we can. Bugs is due to land in Kabul today at twenty hundred hours and will proceed with the handover. In the meantime, we need to get our butts over there. I want you three to be at the RAAF base in Canberra by nineteen hundred tonight. I've arranged a lift for us on a KC-30A transport out of Amberley. It'll detour to Canberra, pick us up from the base at twenty hundred hours, and then fly us direct to Kabul, where we'll rendezvous with Bugs. We'll plan our strategy from there.'

'What about loose ends here ... like Catalina?' Spooky said sharply.

'Apparently she had some help on the inside, so I've put Wyatt and Craig from Charlie team on the case. Being ex-detectives those two should be able to sniff out the mole. They're running checks on all NatSec staff.'

Ben turned to Modeen. 'Have you found any intel that might indicate the mole's identity?'

She rose, went out of the room, and came back holding a bulging bag which she placed on the table in front of him.

'This is everything of any interest that we've found

here so far – their phones, computers and paperwork.' He nodded as she went on. 'And I'd recommend running a background check on one Ivan Singh. He'd be next in line after Baker for the ambassadorship, so we suspect he might be involved in this somehow.'

'Noted. Now, until those checks have been completed this mission remains black ops, and we have to regard everyone in NatSec as being under suspicion and investigation.' Ben paused. 'By the way, good job with Harrison Baker. I caught the item on the evening news. Where have you got him stashed?'

'At my place,' Spooky piped up. 'With Salty keeping an eye on things.'

Ben stared at him thoughtfully. 'I realise you couldn't take him to the safehouse in Canberra, but now he's been incarcerated in your apartment, Spook, you'll have to be relocated.'

He frowned. 'That's a shame. I kinda like that place.'

'Sorry, but we can't risk him finding his way back there.' Ben's tone brooked no argument. 'He can stay there for now, for his own protection. And speaking of safehouses, I'm taking Emily and Chelsea to one in Melbourne.'

Running a hand over his head, he leaned to the side and glanced at where his wife sat bouncing their baby daughter on her knee. 'Just until this is over. I'm not taking any chances after what they've – we've – just been through.' He straightened. 'I'll meet you at the Canberra base at nineteen hundred.'

While Modeen and Spooky nodded their understanding, Wolf frowned. 'But isn't even a safehouse risky considering we have a traitor in the organisation?'

Ben gave a shrewd half smile. 'Let's just say this particular safe house is totally off the radar, and not known to anyone but me.'

'Ah.' Wolf tapped the side of his nose with a finger.

'Now, anything else?' Ben barked. When the others remained quiet, he said, 'Right, the cleaners should be here to mop up within an hour.' He got to his feet with a brisk nod. 'I'll see you in Canberra.'

Striding purposefully into the lounge room, he picked up Chelsea with one arm and put the other around his wife's waist, tucking her against his side. The three of them made their way to the back door and out across the field to the waiting helicopter. Emily stayed close to her husband the whole way and didn't look back.

The Blackhawk rose and thundered away toward Melbourne, as the first hint of dawn nudged the horizon.

After slipping out to retrieve his Aurion from the clearing beside the bridge, Spooky drove it into the driveway of the Porepunkah house. As though in silent agreement the three agents paid their last respects to Gator, and then piled their gear into the car's boot along with what they'd collected from the house. As they were leaving, Wolf stopped and picked up the throwing knives from the floor where he'd dropped them.

He turned to Spooky. 'You have no idea how handy these were, mate.'

Spooky merely nodded and they fist-bumped.

'Yeah.' Modeen stepped closer to Wolf and said awkwardly, 'You … had me worried for a while there. I couldn't see how you were going to get out of that one.'

He reached out and cupped the side of her face in his hand, saying in a gravelly voice, 'And it wasn't easy for me either, seeing you with a knife at your throat.'

'Ahem!' Spooky cleared his throat loudly. 'Well, I guess we'd better make tracks. We've got a transport to Kabul to catch tonight.'

The other two shared a smile and Modeen said matter-of-factly, 'Right, I'll call Salty and give him a sit-rep.'

———

Catalina woke early and sat up in bed, naked except for a pair of flannelette pyjama bottoms. Tossing back her tousled mane of dark hair, she grabbed the mobile phone from the bedside table and checked the screen.

No update text messages since before three am.

Scowling, she took a wary glance at the sleeping form beside her and then swung her legs off the edge of the bed. After dialling a number in her contacts list she leaned forward, pressed the phone to her ear, and listened intently.

Her call wasn't answered.

She tried another number.

Same result.

Her frown deepened. Clicking off the phone, she sat staring at it and chewing a fingernail. After a few minutes, she reached over to shake the young man lying beside her. It took a bit to wake him and when he did stir, it was with an irritated grimace.

Putting a hand to his head, he squeezed his puffy eyes shut and moaned, 'What?'

'I need you to go into work early,' she rapped, 'and check what's going on.'

'What?' he grumbled again, blinking at her. 'What time is it?' He pulled the bedclothes higher, clearly unwilling to comply.

She narrowed her eyes at him, and in a cat-like movement straddled him in the bed. 'Come on, it's not that early.' Pulling back the sheets, she ran a long fingernail down his bare chest. 'By the time we have a shower and get dressed it'll be seven o'clock.'

He stared at her, bleary-eyed and unimpressed. 'Seven? Are you crazy? I don't normally start work 'til eight-thirty.'

'Please?' Catalina wheedled, leaning lower so her

breasts brushed against him. 'I need to know that everything's alright.'

His breath quickened. 'OK, but the guy coming off night shift is going to wonder why I'm in so early.'

When he reached for her, she sat up.

'Thanks, babe.' Taking hold of his hands she leapt off the bed, ignoring his grumbles. 'C'mon, you need a shower.'

'What I need,' he said sourly as she pulled him upright, 'is to take it easier on the booze and … the stuff.' He rubbed his head. 'It feels great at the time, but I feel like crap afterwards.'

'Don't be a sook!' She led him, stumbling, into the bathroom. 'And *I* know best what you need….'

Forty minutes later he was dressed and standing beside her in the doorway.

Snaking her arms around his neck, she put her lips to his ear. 'Call me as soon as you know anything.' She tucked a small package into his hand, murmuring, 'This'll help you feel better.'

He stared at the package with an uncertain frown, but then tucked it carefully into his pocket. 'Meet you at the café, usual time?'

'Sure. And don't forget to call me as soon as you know anything.' Pushing him into the hallway, she blew him a token kiss as she shut the door.

———

Staring dubiously at Spooky's espresso machine, Salty pulled a face. He went to the corner pantry and scanned the shelves, giving a pleased sigh when he found a jar of Nescafe instant coffee. Mumbling, 'Good ol' forty-three beans in every cup,' he put the kettle on and popped slices of bread into the toaster. While waiting for the water to boil, he scratched around in the cupboards and found a tray.

Whistling an old tune, he busied himself cutting a wedge of butter. Putting it on a saucer, he set it on the tray beside a jar of Vegemite, a butter knife, two cups of coffee, and finally the bits of toast on a plate.

Still whistling he carried the tray down the corridor, unlocked Baker's door and entered the room.

Seeing Baker sitting up in the bed he said cheerfully, 'Mornin',' as he placed the tray on the side table.

Taking one of the cups of coffee for himself he perched on the end of the bed, took a sip, and grinned at Baker. 'There's more toast if you're still hungry after this lot.'

Baker glanced at the tray and grunted, but then his expression changed and he sat forward. Flicking back the bedclothes, he whipped out a hand to grab the butter knife. Pointing it threateningly at Salty, he gave a wicked grin and snarled, 'Not too clever, are we? Let's see how brave you are now I'm armed.'

When Salty spluttered into laughter, spitting coffee everywhere, Baker frowned at him. It wasn't the reaction he'd expected.

Swallowing his mirth long enough to blow a raspberry, Salty reached behind and chortled, 'You ever heard that ol' saying, Baker, about takin' a knife to a gun fight?'

Pulling the Glock from the back of his pants, he gave another bark of laughter. ''Cept I don't think *that*,' and he pointed the pistol's muzzle at the butter knife in Baker's hand, 'even counts as a knife.'

Baker pouted and sagged, dropping the butter knife back on the tray with a clatter.

Salty grinned at him. 'I've gotta hand it to ya for tryin', son. You're not a quitter, that's for sure.' He tucked the Glock back into his pants. 'Anyways, looks like you'll be here for a couple more days, so why not sit back and enjoy bein' pampered by yours truly.'

Baker scowled. 'A couple of days?'

'Like I said, son, it's for your own safety. And your family's.'

'My safety?' Baker sniffed, irately jabbing both index fingers at the bandage around his head. 'What-d'ya call *this*?'

Salty's expression grew serious. 'That'll heal,' he said. 'Besides, it could be worse. You could be dead.'

———

Catalina jumped when her phone chimed. Grabbing it, she puffed, 'Yes, what've you found out?'

'Nothing's wrong,' the voice said at the other end of

the phone. 'He's not in his office this morning, as you expected. Three of his agents flew to Canberra yesterday, and the other one is on his way to Kabul. That's a sixteen hour flight to Dubai followed by another two hours fifty after a five hour stopover. Apart from that, no other itineraries or resources have been logged through our system.'

Hearing that, Catalina gave an anxious click of her tongue.

'Meet you at the café as planned?' her caller asked hopefully, but the phone went silent.

The young man stared at his mobile for a long moment before putting it down on his desk. Looking up, he gave a start at the sight of two agents standing on the other side of his cubicle staring down at him with grim expressions.

'Reece Riley?' Wyatt raised his eyebrows and Reece gave a tentative nod. The agents moved to stand on either side of him as Craig took his arm saying, 'You need to come with us.'

They were engrossed in their own thoughts for most of the trip back to Canberra. Wolf sat up front with Spooky, and Modeen had opted for the middle of the rear bench seat.

As they approached a tavern on the city's outskirts, Wolf barked, 'Pull in here for some breakfast ... lunch ... er, whatever. I'm hungry.'

With a quick glance in the rear-view mirror, Spooky veered the Aurion into the outside lane. As they pulled into the tavern's carpark, Modeen reached an arm between the front seats and touched Wolf on a brawny shoulder. Her voice was just above a whisper when she said, 'I'm sorry.'

'What for?' Both men turned to stare at her quizzically.

'I should've shot ... him ... as soon as I saw he was armed,' she said miserably. 'If I'd done that I could've taken care of the giant and the guard on the top landing as well. Instead I kicked the gun out of his hand and that put you, Spooky, and Emily at unnecessary risk. I could've compromised the whole outcome.'

'That's crap,' Wolf barked. 'You gave him a chance, it's not your fault he didn't take it. He could've thrown down right there and then but he chose instead to force our hands.'

Spooky chimed in. 'Yeah, hindsight's a wonderful thing but don't go second guessing your actions.' His tone grew solemn. 'And don't forget it was Gator you were dealing with, not some random goon. We wouldn't have expected you to act any differently.'

She turned angst-ridden eyes onto him. 'But I put you in a situation where you had to shoot an army buddy of ours, someone who'd been like family to us.'

'It came down to him or you, so there was no contest. By his actions he took the decision out of our hands. Don't beat yourself up about it.' He stuck out his chin. 'I'm not.'

'Come on,' Wolf drawled, giving her hand a squeeze. 'Let's get some tucker.' As they walked across the carpark he pulled her close against his side and kissed her on the temple.

She gave him a wan smile and then reached across to bump Spooky on the shoulder with her fist. 'By the way, thanks Spook. I owe you.'

––––––––

Sitting in the main lounge at Dubai airport, Bugs tapped on his phone and placed it to his ear. 'K-man, how'd you get on? Did you and Anthony get time off?'

'Yeah mate, not a problem.' Karim spoke with a heavy Australian accent. 'We put in for a couple of days R-n-R and our CO didn't even bat an eyelid. I reckon your guy must've pulled a few strings.'

'That's great, 'cos it looks like I'm gonna need you for a couple of days. Any chance you could bring my Humvee to the airport and pick me up?'

'Shouldn't be a problem. What time?'

'My plane's due in at thirteen hundred hours.'

Karim grunted.

'The code for the gate is still the same,' Bugs continued, 'and the keys are in the usual spot. Make sure the tool kit's full, we've got a job to do on the way home.'

'Right-o.'

Bugs hung up and then tapped his phone again.

Modeen answered on the second ring.

'Hey Bugs.'

'Hey. So, how'd you get on?'

'All good. We got Emily and Chelsea back safe and unharmed. Ben's taken them to Melbourne. After that he's going to rendezvous with us here in Canberra.'

'How did you guys fare, are you all OK?'

'Yeah, but Gator....' Modeen paused and took a breath. 'We had to neutralise him, Bugs.'

'Oh.'

After a moment's silence she said, 'I'll fill you in on the details when we get there.'

'You're coming here?'

'Yep.'

'Just you?'

'No, all four of us. We're leaving at twenty hundred hours tonight, flying straight to Kabul on a KC-30A transport Ben's organised. They reckon it should only take about fourteen hours flying time. With a range of over fourteen thousand kilometres, those things don't even have to stop to refuel.'

'Yeah, they're basically a modified A330 Airbus. The RAAF has five of 'em and they regularly rotate out of Bagram airbase. Anyway, have you got any further orders or intel for me?'

'Not at this stage. Ben confirmed he wants you to proceed as planned, and we'll join you there ASAP.'

'I've got the K-man and Anthony to give me a hand with the release. They're both out of the Second Commando Regiment based here in Kabul, and just back from a mission.'

'Good. We don't know yet what we're up against, so extra muscle will probably come in handy.'

'Looks like I'll be landing in Kabul shortly before you take off from Canberra. So after I've handed over ol' mate, do you just want me to "hang" 'til you get here?'

Modeen laughed. 'Yeah Bugs, just "hang", but monitor Akim's movements. Don't engage unless you have to. You'll be able to contact us while we're in the air so call us if you need to. Ben will no doubt be in touch with you soon. Good luck with your mission.'

'Cheers, seeya soon.' Bugs ended the call.

——————

'We'll be there in about fifteen, Salty.' To his ears, Modeen's voice sounded metallic through the mobile's speakers. 'Is there anything you want us to pick up for you?'

'No thanks, lovely lady, I'm OK,' Salty replied. 'But I wouldn't mind nippin' out to stretch my legs before you head off again.'

'Not a problem. We'll see you shortly.'

Wolf extended a hand to Salty as they entered the apartment. 'Hey, old mate.'

'Humph.' Salty shook his large paw firmly and said with a wry grin, 'How about we keep age out of this?'

'Nah, I kinda like being called "youngster".' Wolf threw him a wink as Modeen and Spooky piled in behind him.

Salty greeted them cheerfully. 'It's good to see you guys back in one piece. Well done on getting Ben's family back safely.'

After they'd settled in the lounge room and given

Salty a full run-down, Spooky inclined his head toward the locked bedroom door. 'How's our guest?'

'Alright, but getting a bit sick of pizza. Can't blame him, to be honest. Thought I'd go out and get some supplies … might even do him a good turn and make some of Salty Dick's famous chowder, assuming I can get some reasonable seafood down here.'

Modeen smiled. 'Bugs mentioned that you were a bit of a wizard with the seafood.'

'Did he now?' Salty gave a proud grin. 'He was sceptical at first, but once he tried my seafood chowder and mud crab combo, the boy was hooked.'

Wolf licked his lips. 'Ya got me.'

'Unfortunately,' Modeen cut in, 'we have to be at the airport by nineteen hundred, so we won't be able to stay for dinner.'

She ignored Wolf's muttered protest and continued. 'We'll leave a bit earlier and grab something to eat on the way there. Thanks, by the way, for helping us out with Baker, Salty. Has he been behaving himself?'

Salty nodded. 'He's got a bit of spunk for a politician, I'm impressed.' He chuckled. 'Nothing I can't handle, of course. And I've changed the dressing on his scalp. The wound's healing nicely.'

'Good.' Modeen gave a satisfied nod. 'Thanks for taking care of things for us.'

'Anytime. So, you guys are off to Afghanistan … tonight.' Salty glanced around at the three of them.

'Ben's determined to tie up any loose ends,'

Modeen explained. 'He believes the SoA's nest is in Kabul, so he wants to follow-up on leads over there. He's also organised some background checks on Ivan Singh, the guy who would've stepped up if anything had happened to Baker.' She got to her feet and looked down at Salty.

'I guess Ben won't want Baker released until we're finished in Afghanistan, and once he's certain there's no further threat.'

'I know how these thing go, and I'm happy to help any way I can.' Salty paused. 'And if I were Ben, I'd be doin' the same thing. Bet he's feelin' like a lucky man, gettin' his family back safe and sound.' He gave a slow nod of his head. 'Yep, I can understand why he'd want to put an end to all this strife.'

CHAPTER FOURTEEN

'Stay on Pialligo for now, then turn left onto Scherger Drive. The RAAF hangar is around the back of the airport in Point Cook Avenue.' Spooky called out directions from the back seat of the Aurion.

Modeen made the left turn into Scherger Drive and was moving parallel with the main airfield runway when she checked the rear-view mirror. 'This'll be Ben now,' she announced.

Wolf leaned forward to check the passenger's side mirror and Spooky craned his neck to peer out the back window. They both reacted automatically, ducking their heads when a Sikorsky Blackhawk helicopter thundered over the top of them, making the car shake.

Modeen turned into Point Cook Avenue and stopped the car in front of the RAAF hangar.

The helicopter had landed nearby and was

powering down, its turbo engines whining as the main rotor slowed and the blades tilted downward.

As they watched, Ben jumped down from the chopper.

He was dressed in desert camouflage fatigues, and to Modeen's eyes, looked decidedly relaxed considering the stress he'd been through. Keeping his head down, he jogged across the tarmac to where they stood on the apron.

They nodded greetings and Spooky said, 'Should I bring the Aurion around and unload the boot?'

'No need.' Ben shook his head. 'I've arranged for a fully kitted-out vehicle to be waiting for us in Kabul.'

Wolf raised a dark eyebrow. 'I hope they kit it out with better gear than that crap Robson gave us last time.'

'Yeah,' Spooky said, 'I'd rather take our own equipment if that's the case.'

Ben gave a lopsided grin. 'Robson's OK, and he's certainly redeemed himself on this mission. He's had to pull strings and step on toes to get our transport diverted from Amberley. It wasn't due to fly to Kabul until next week so they had to change flight plans and re-schedule crews. Besides, he's a wing commander so providing small arms isn't really his forte.'

'Well at least we agree on that.' Wolf thumped Ben's shoulder with a fist. 'How are Emily and Chelsea, did you get them squared away?'

'They're in good spirits, considering.' He was interrupted by the twin engines of the Blackhawk whirring back into life. As the helicopter rose into the air, giving the runway a wide berth, Ben gathered his agents in tight for a pre-mission briefing.

———

At thirteen fifteen Bugs stepped off the United Emirates A343 Airbus into a pleasant twenty-nine degrees and a cloudless sky. It was a typical early June day in the desert climate of Kabul.

A large bearded man stood in front of the airport with his arms crossed, staring into the arrivals lounge. At six foot four and dressed in desert camouflage fatigues and wearing dark aviator sunglasses, Karim's muscular physique made an imposing impression on passers-by. People leaving the building gave him a wide berth, avoiding making eye contact as they scurried past. He didn't move as Bugs walked up to stand in front of him.

'K-man!' He flashed a toothy grin. 'Good to see ya, buddy.' Extending a hand, he shook Karim's large paw.

'Bugs.' Karim nodded. 'Mate, I thought you were going to be in Oz for a coupl'a months?'

'So did I.' Bugs gave a shrug. 'But it appears there is some urgent business that requires my full attention.' The two men started walking toward the carpark.

Keeping his voice low, Karim said, 'I dropped Tony off at the coordinates you gave me.'

'Is he any good, this Tony? I haven't worked with him before.'

'A bit full of himself,' Karim said, rubbing his beard, 'and something of a stirrer. Most of the time he's pretty sullen and anti-social.'

'So, a good sniper then.' Bugs dug him in the ribs and Karim gave a deep chuckle.

'You said it.'

'Well,' Bugs said thoughtfully, 'if they stick to the plan, he should only have to cover us from six hundred metres. A walk in the park for an average sniper. Did he take the Vanquish?'

'Nah, said he'd prefer to use his SR98. It's fitted with a screw-on suppressor and is effective at eight hundred metres, so should do just fine.'

'OK. Anyway, he's only there for back-up, so he may not need to fire a shot.'

'He won't like that,' Karim muttered, heading through the rows of parked vehicles. 'Your Humvee is locked and loaded as requested.' Raising a brawny arm, he pointed to the rear of the carpark.

The military Humvee with its desert camouflage paint job looked like the business on a frame of just over two metres wide and just below two metres tall. It dwarfed the other, insignificant-looking domestic vehicles around it. And when Bugs started its six and a half litre turbo diesel engine, the motor rumbled impressively into life. Putting it into gear, he nosed the Humvee out of the parking bay and then roared out of the carpark, heading toward Eggers base near the US embassy.

Bugs drove up to the boom gates and flashed his NatSec ID. 'Barry Peterson, to see Major Cody Braden.'

The guard glanced over at Karim who held up his Australian Defence Force ID. 'Wait here.' Disappearing into the booth, the guard spoke briefly on the phone and then re-emerged. 'Continue on, then take a right turn at the back of the compound. The major is in the last building on the left.' As he spoke, the guard raised the boom gate and they drove through.

Parking near the building, they strode into its small reception area and remained standing, hands behind their backs, while they waited. Major Cody Braden appeared a few minutes later and greeted them curtly before escorting them to the detention compound within the base. As they walked, Bugs took in the ten foot high weldmesh fencing capped with spiralled razor wire that surrounded the smaller inner compound.

Braden flicked them a glance and muttered, 'You're welcome to this prick. As far as we're concerned he's small fry.'

'Well, he might not be on your radar,' Bugs replied, 'but he's certainly come up as a blip on ours.'

'Yeah, well Akim's out of action now, isn't he,' Braden went on drily, 'and he's the least of our worries at present. The US Embassy has been attacked for the second time this month, and now two female journalists have gone missing, assumed taken by rebel forces.' He held up a battle-hardened, scarred hand and spread his fingers. 'There are about five different factions here that we know of, six if you include this idiot and his followers.' He sighed. 'On one hand the civilians here are begging us to stay, and on the other we're confronted by a new terrorist group just about every month.'

Glancing over his shoulder at them, he shook his head. 'It's crazy, there are four million people here in Afghanistan but the terrorist numbers seem to be burgeoning. It's like they're flooding back home from all over the world to join the mayhem.' He looked forward again. 'The good thing is, when they're not attacking us or innocent civilians, they're usually fighting amongst themselves trying to exert their dominance.'

When Braden stopped abruptly, Bugs looked down the long fenced corridor ahead and saw a slightly-built man dressed in bright orange overalls shuffling toward them flanked by two heavily armed US marines. The man's arms and legs were shackled with chains and he looked morose as he lumbered, head down, toward them.

Braden turned to Bugs. 'The guards will escort him to your vehicle.'

Bugs shook his hand. 'Thanks, major.'

'Well, he's all yours.' Braden took a moment to also shake Karim's hand before nodding at both men and striding back toward his office.

The two guards didn't speak as they walked Saddam Akim to Bug's Humvee. When they got there, Karim stepped forward and clamped a huge hand on Akim's shoulder. Practically lifting him into the back seat, he nudged Akim over with his hip and sat down next to him.

Bugs thanked the guards and jumped into the driver's seat. He checked his watch.

Right on time.

Starting the Humvee, he drove south to Qala Zaman Khan Road and then pulled off the road into a clearing. Getting out of the vehicle, he walked around to the far side, opened the rear door, and slammed a fist into the right side of Akim's face.

When Akim's head rocked back against Karim's arm, Bugs took something from his pocket and leaned inside. He indicated the unconscious man with a lift of his chin. 'Open his mouth.'

Grabbing a handful of Akim's hair, Karim reefed his head back and down and Akim's mouth fell open. Bugs held up a small device and flicked it down the back of Akim's throat, after which he took a bottle of water from off the floor and poured some into his mouth. Akim spluttered and regained consciousness with a start, spluttering and coughing violently.

'You OK now, mate?' Karim gave him a couple of

pats on the side of his face and was rewarded with a furious pout and more coughing.

Bugs climbed back into the driver's seat and steered the Humvee along Maranjan Hill Road, where hectares of land had been cleared in preparation for a new residential subdivision. In the distance a huge hill skirted the northern side of the development. Slowing the Humvee, Bugs pulled off the road and drove along a gravel track until they reached a vast clearing, where a black Rolls Royce sat waiting.

'Nice ride,' Karim mumbled from the back seat. 'Check out the chrome grille. It's got one of those figure heads … you know, the winged woman leaning into a stiff breeze.'

'Yeah.' Bugs gave an appreciative nod. 'A "Spirit of Ecstasy", that's what they're called. And this one's crystal by the looks of it. Pretty impressive.'

Beside Karim, Akim roused himself and gave a triumphant smirk.

When Bugs parked the Humvee ten metres back from the limousine, three guerrillas with AK47s emerged. They were followed by a fat, black-suited man who reached up to wipe his florid face with a handkerchief. The sun glinted off the gold rings on his pudgy fingers and a cigar hung from the corner of his mouth.

Grabbing an M4 Carbine, Karim opened the door and dragged their charge out of the back seat. Standing beside his huge guard, Akim looked like a pathetic, skinny weasel. Bugs took the lead and the three of them marched toward the limousine.

At their approach, the man in the suit sauntered over to meet them halfway. Seeing him, Akim straightened and puffed out his chest, trying to look more dignified as he shuffled next to Karim.

The man stopped and said in guttural English, 'Very good. It is pleasing to see that you are cooperating.' His eyes narrowed until they were mere slits in his oval face. 'We have been unable to communicate with our friends in Australia. What do you know of this?'

Bugs gave a nonchalant shrug of his broad shoulders. 'We're just the delivery boys.' Turning, he gestured at Akim. 'We've been ordered to bring you this piece of sh—' Stopping, he gave an unrepentant, toothy grin. 'To bring you your ... comrade.'

Akim stumbled forward as Karim nudged him with the butt of his assault rifle. Drawing him into a hug, the man in the suit gave a curt nod and then walked Akim toward the limousine.

As Bugs and Karim turned to go back to the Humvee, the man gave a hand signal and three guerrillas stepped forward and levelled their weapons.

At a faint hiss above their heads, Bugs and Karim whipped around in time to see the Spirit of Ecstasy explode in a shower of crystal fragments across the Roller's highly-polished bonnet.

The guerrillas ducked, covering their faces and

lowering their weapons. Peering up at the ridge over six hundred and fifty metres away, and then at Bugs and Karim, they backed toward the limousine and got in, slamming the doors behind them.

The car was already moving, its tyres spinning and throwing up gravel as the driver accelerated hard and sped back toward the main road.

'Right,' Bugs said, slapping his hands together, 'that's done. Reckon it's your shout, K-man, and your mate Tony deserves a drink after that.'

CHAPTER FIFTEEN

Climbing into the Humvee, Bugs and Karim headed back the way they'd come. They turned off Qala Zaman Khan Road and skirted along the top of the ridge overlooking the subdivision.

Bugs nosed the vehicle onto the edge of the ridge and stopped. Looking across the valley where they had delivered Saddam Akim, he re-checked the GPS and muttered, 'These are the coordinates.'

Beside him, Karim pointed to the nose of the vehicle as a tall, rangy man in army fatigues emerged from the foliage in front of them.

Draping a camouflage blanket over his shoulder and carrying a sniper rifle, the man jogged to the Humvee and jumped into the back seat, grumbling, 'For a moment there I thought you were gonna run over me.'

Bugs flashed him a grin. 'Nice shot.' He stretched

his right arm over the bench seat. 'Barry, or you can call me Bugs.'

'Tony.' They shook hands and Tony started wiping the camouflage paint from his face. 'I wasn't too sure what the protocol was in that situation, so thought I'd just scare the crap out of 'em.'

'You did just fine.' Bugs eyed both the men. 'I've got my old unit flying in at o-two hundred tomorrow. You two OK to meet me at my pad around then?'

They nodded their agreement and Tony stopped wiping his face to ask, 'Isn't Ben Logan in your unit?'

'Yep.'

'And he's coming here?'

'Sure is. Do you know him?'

'Not personally, but I think everyone in the service knows about him and his squad, and how he got his VC. But I thought he'd retired?'

'Well, sort of retired.' Bugs chose his words carefully. 'Every now and then they pull him out of mothballs just to keep his hand in.'

Tony nodded and was about to resume wiping his face when his eyes lit up and he said enthusiastically, 'Say that sheila, the first one to join the SASR – Modeen I think her name is – is she coming here too?'

Bugs threw him an amused glance. 'Easy there, mate. I wouldn't be puttin' any moves on Modeen if I were you.'

'Why not? She's not in the force anymore.' Tony sat forward, a challenge in his sharp, blue-grey eyes. 'And she's one good-lookin' babe.' His voice deepened and his expression grew lustful. 'Your motto was "who dares wins", right? I might borrow it.'

'Sure, but in this case "who dares" would lose and find himself bein' torn a new one by the Wolf.'

'Wolf? You mean Troy Wolverton?' Tony sat back. 'I've heard about him too. Meant to've got the longest kill for a sniper, almost twenty-five hundred metres using a fifty cal Barrett. Unfortunately for him, it wasn't officially recorded.' A cocky note crept into his voice. 'So I reckon it might've been either a fluke, or exaggerated a little. 'N maybe the same goes for him 'n Modeen.'

'Think what you like,' Bugs said dismissively, throwing Karim a wink. 'You can take that up with Wolf when he gets here. But one thing I *can* tell you for certain is that the shot you're talking about, if it was a fluke like you reckon, Wolf managed to pull it off twice. I was spottin' for him that day, here in Afghanistan. He took out two Taliban insurgents, both at over twenty-four hundred metres.' Flicking Tony a sideways glance, he said firmly, 'And the targets weren't sitting on their arses either, they were mobile at the time.'

Turning to the front again, Bugs tapped on his phone and checked his tracking app. A blue dot was south of their location and heading south-east on Esteolal Road. He frowned and murmured, 'It could be a long night, so I suggest you guys get some sleep if you can. You can crash at my place if you like.' His eyes brightened. 'Think I've even got a few beers in the fridge.'

———

Ben gazed up at the Royal Australian Air Force KC-30A multi-role transport as it approached the runway.

Beside him Modeen idly mused that the aircraft's light colour, the standard 'Air Force grey', somehow helped the big plane blend into its surroundings.

'That thing can carry a hundred tonnes of fuel?' Spooky murmured.

'Yeah,' Wolf drawled, 'the RAAF uses it for air-to-air refuelling and strategic transport.'

They watched as it touched down with puffs of smoke from its eight undercarriage tyres, the huge General Electric turbofan engines beneath each wing roaring as it braked hard before taxiing off the runway toward the RAAF hangar.

Canberra airport ground crew hastened to roll out a set of aluminium stairs as the marshaller signalled the pilot, guiding him to a stop next to the hangar. As the stairs touched the fuselage, the plane's door opened. When a RAAF crewman motioned for them to board, Ben and his team climbed the steps and entered the plane.

After the ground crew had conducted visual checks of the undercarriage, the stairs were removed and the door closed. The marshaller took up position in front of the aircraft and signalled to the pilot as the huge jet began taxiing back out onto the runway.

Inside, Ben and his team settled themselves for the long trip. Between them and the eight staff on board, including the pilot and co-pilot, the plane felt empty and eerily deserted.

The front of its interior was decked out like a normal A330 airliner, but instead of the usual row upon row of three hundred-odd seats, there were only ten rows. Modeen and Wolf sat on the front left side, taking a whole row each so they could stretch out, and Ben and Spooky did the same on the right.

'I hope we get inflight service,' Spooky said doubtfully as the jet accelerated down the runway and they were pushed back in their seats.

Fifteen minutes into the flight, Ben's phone vibrated with an incoming message.

SA released, TD5035.

———

Salty knocked on the door as a courtesy before unlocking it and entering Baker's room to collect his dishes.

'So, Harrison,' he said cheerily, 'how'd you like Salty's chowder?'

'It was alright I guess.' Baker sat leaning against the headboard.

Eyeing the empty plate on the serving tray, Salty thought it looked suspiciously like it had been licked clean. Swallowing a pleased grin, he retrieved the tray and raised bushy grey eyebrows at Baker.

'If you prefer, we can go back to having pizza?'

Baker gave him a look and muttered, 'Chowder will be fine.'

'Good.' Salty smiled. 'Well, with a bit of luck you'll be out of here within the next couple of days.'

Crossing his arms over his chest, Baker grumbled, 'Fat lot of good that's doing my family.' He stared moodily at the floor.

Salty gave a dubious frown. 'They'd be worried about you for sure, but it's not like you've been gone long. And knowing the guys helpin' you – and yes, they're on your side even if you don't believe that – you'll be back with your family soon.'

He eyed Baker thoughtfully and then sat on the end of the bed. 'I know you're the replacement ambassador for Afghanistan, but what did you do to get your name on a hit list?'

'Nothing.' Baker pouted and threw his hands in the air. 'That's what I don't understand.'

'Mm.' Salty's eyes narrowed. 'So, what were your plans for when you took up your new position?'

Baker stuck out his chin. 'There's a lot of corruption in Afghanistan, and some in upper level government suspect it's tainting our operations over there. If that's true, I've been commissioned with putting a stop to it, to clean up our act.'

Salty nodded. 'I see. And you're quite open about telling people that? I guess you must be if you're telling me.'

'Well it's the truth,' Baker huffed. 'Everyone knows the Afghani government's reputation. The US alone gave them over a hundred billion dollars to rebuild their war-torn city, but most of the funds have disappeared, victim of wide-spread graft and corruption.'

Seeing Baker sit forward, warming to his subject, Salty took advantage of his chattiness. 'So, tell me about this Singh bloke?'

'Ivan? He graduated with honours in a Bachelor of Business from Curtin University, and rose quickly through the government ranks,' Baker announced proudly. 'I've been teaching him the ropes. He's a quick learner and very keen.'

'What do you know of his background?'

'I'm not sure.' Baker's brow creased. 'With a name like Singh he must have Middle-eastern roots.' He paused and then said pompously as though reading from some PR boffin's spin, 'But we're a multi-cultural country and don't judge people by their origins, if that's what you're getting at.'

Salty raised an eyebrow and got to his feet. 'No, not at all. Live 'n let live, that's my motto.' He bent to collect the tray. 'But it might be prudent to do proper background checks on the people "rising quickly through the ranks", to make sure we aren't standing blithely by while terrorists or their supporters infiltrate our government.' With that, he left an open-mouthed Baker staring after him as he strode out of the room, locking the door behind him.

Back in the kitchen he stacked the dirty dishes into the dishwasher, grabbed a beer from the fridge and flicked on the TV, mumbling under his breath, 'Freakin' pompous pollies.'

CHAPTER SIXTEEN

Running a tired hand over her face and licking her dry lips, Catalina Hernandez tried to work out how long it had been since she'd last eaten or drunk anything. Quite a few hours, she decided, and that was why she now felt parched and hollow.

But food and drink had been the last things on her mind.

Unable to contact her colleagues or get any useful information from her NatSec informant, she had jumped in her car and driven from Melbourne to Canberra via Porepunkah in a state of high tension. She'd earned herself a speeding ticket along the way, having foolishly allowed anxiety to affect her usual caution. Her outrage and frustration at that had only added to her tension. And her arrival at the Crystal Brook Avenue property hadn't done anything to ease her anxiety.

In fact, it took her to the verge of panic.

She had found the house deserted and more worryingly, wiped clean. That was wrong on every level. For one, there should've been a bunch of people there. Even if they'd had to relocate for some reason she would've been notified of their movements. And for another thing, the types of goons they used weren't neat, tidy, house-trained individuals. But there'd been no rubbish lying around, no overflowing ashtrays stinking up the rooms, no used but unflushed toilets or taps left dripping, no vehicles in the garage, no sign they'd been there at all.

And yet she knew they had.

She had noticed some new hinges on the doors and what appeared to be repairs to an upstairs window. But had they been like that beforehand? She couldn't be sure....

Parking her Hyundai i30 and turning off the lights, she pulled out her mobile and called her contact in Afghanistan. As soon as he answered she announced breathlessly, 'The Porepunkah property was deserted, no sign of Crockman or the others. It's ... it's as if they were never there.'

'This is most unusual,' the heavily accented voice at the other end of the international call said smoothly. 'However, the infidels appear to be holding up their end of the deal. Saddam Akim is here with me now. He has been released to us and this "Baker" person has been eliminated.'

She heard the squeak of new leather and the click of a lighter, followed by the sound of a cigar being lit, sucked, and the smoke exhaled. And when he smacked his lips and spoke again, she could imagine Akeem Jibril reclining in the leather seat of his much loved Rolls Royce, a self-satisfied look on his swarthy face.

'If Crockman and the others have met with foul play,' he said calmly, 'it is of no consequence to us here. They have served their purpose, we have no further need of them.'

'But—'

'Leave it, Catalina. It is time for you to come home.'

The call ended with an abrupt click and she lowered the phone.

Gazing up at a multi-storey apartment complex in Canberra's inner city, she chewed her lower lip and contemplated her next move.

It was almost ten pm and condensation quickly formed on the car's windows, fogging them thickly.

One part of her mind was telling her to drive away, to follow Jibril's instructions and leave the country. But another was urging her to find out what had happened to Crockman and the prisoners. If she could tie up those loose ends, she might be allowed to stay in Australia and take control of activities there.

At that thought, her dark eyes narrowed greedily and she ran the tip of her tongue over her grinning lips. Gut instinct told her that Luke Williams would know exactly what was going on. And she knew where he lived….

Taking a deep breath she rolled her shoulders, opened the door, and stepped into the chilly night air.

Salty reclined on the lounge chair, a beer at his elbow, gazing at the television. When the evening news came on, he turned up the volume.

'Rebel attacks continue in Kabul, Afghanistan's capital,' the newsreader announced. 'A media crew has been set upon in the city and two American journalists are missing, assumed taken by rebel forces. Sharon Harris and Sally Cockburn were on their first overseas assignment.'

Photographs of two pretty blonde women appeared on the screen. 'As yet, no rebel faction has claimed responsibility.'

Salty leaned forward to take a closer look when there was a knock on the door. Wondering who would be calling so late in the day, he got up to peer through the peep hole to see a shapely brunette outside the door. She was on her own and standing side-on so he could only see her in profile, but it was a nice profile. And his nose caught a hint of her musky perfume wafting under the door.

Thinking, *Hmm … Spooky has a good-looking visitor,* he gave a snort. *Well, he is a single bloke.*

Realising she could probably hear the TV from out in the corridor, he decided it would be rude to ignore her.

Better not spoil the youngster's chances.

He tucked his shirt into his pants and ran a hand over his hair. *I'll tell her he's away and suggest she call him in a few days.*

When he opened the door a crack, she whirled around and he got his first proper look at her. Recognition dawned on his face and he frowned. *'You?'*

Without a word she shoved the door open and kicked him squarely in the chest. He fell backwards and used the momentum to roll full circle and spring to his feet.

Surprised by the old man's agility, Catalina stepped into the room after him, throwing a left and then a right cross, both of which he deflected.

As he stepped forward, about to mount an offensive of his own, he saw her gasp and wince as her head was wrenched violently back by the hair. At the same time a Glock was thrust into the side of her face. She gave a furious yelp and then froze as two men materialised on either side of her and grabbed her by the arms.

Pulling her hands behind her back and snapping handcuffs on her wrists, Craig looked over at Salty. 'You OK?'

'Only just gettin' warmed up, youngster.' Salty said, glancing at their ID cards. 'You NatSec?'

He nodded. 'I'm Craig, and this is Wyatt.'

'Good to meet ya. So, how'd you know where to find her?'

'We were ordered to run background checks on all agency staff which led us to this one.' Craig indicated Catalina with a lift of his chin. 'We've been monitoring her movements since finding out how *friendly* she'd become with a young lad at HQ in Melbourne.'

'Yeah,' Salty muttered, 'she's good at that.' Glancing at Catalina, he gave a syrupy grin. 'Well, thanks for droppin' by, *Cat*. That's what Luke called you, isn't it?'

And as the agents escorted her to the door he called, 'Shame you can't stay.'

She threw him a livid glance, her pretty face twisting and turning ugly as she was unceremoniously bundled out the door.

———

Bugs slowed the Humvee and pulled up in front of a pair of eight foot gates within the fenced Aussie expat compound that had been his home for the past two years. Karim jumped out of the passenger's side of the vehicle, punched a code into the oversized lock that linked the gates together, and swung them open.

As he nosed the Humvee through the gateway, Bugs pressed the remote control he'd clipped to the sun visor and the roller door on his zincalume garage began to rattle open. Leaving Karim to close and lock the gates again, Bugs drove forward and carefully nudged the wide vehicle into the garage.

It was a tight fit so Tony had to squeeze out of the back door. Moments later Karim hustled in behind the Humvee as the roller door rattled back down.

'Make yourselves at home,' Bugs said as he let them into his living quarters. 'You can toss a coin for who gets the spare bed and who gets the sofa. There's tea and coffee in the pantry, and some beers in the fridge. We've got about thirteen hours to kill and I'm feelin' jet-lagged, so I'm gonna grab some shut-eye.'

Tony glanced around the small two bedroom unit. It was modern and, unlike the traditional Afghani mud brick house, he knew it would have at least a flushing toilet, shower, and a tap over the sink. With the look of a typical bachelor's pad, its open plan had a cluttered kitchen at one end and an untidy living area at the other.

A three-seater sofa, covered in car magazines, food wrappers and stubby cubbies, separated the kitchen from the living area and was angled to face the huge flat screen TV dominating one corner of the living room. In the opposite corner a double-stack home gym, complete with leg press and assorted dumbbells, took up the rest of the usable space.

'I'm feelin' pretty pumped,' Tony said, as he flicked through Bugs' collection of DVDs. 'Reckon I might do a workout. Then I'll have one of his beers, put on a movie and chill out.'

In the kitchen, busy trying to find some food and a clean cup to make himself a coffee, Karim merely grunted.

———

The black Rolls Royce drove south on the Kabul-Gardez Highway. Inside, one of its occupants gazed out the window at the distant mountain range, a scenic backdrop to the L-shape of lake Hashmat Khan.

'Ahh,' he sighed, 'it is good to be home and free again.' Turning to smile at the man beside him, he raised his hands in a gesture of gratitude, making his shackles jangle. 'Thank you, my friend.'

He was awarded with a clap on the shoulder from a gold be-ringed hand and a grunted, 'It is nothing. And we will soon rid you of those restraints.'

Nodding and returning his gaze to the mountains, the man's dark eyes followed the line of the range which extended well beyond the wetland marshes to the south.

As the limousine passed the range's southernmost point at Beni Hisar, the driver turned right off the highway onto a narrow, semi-sealed road. They continued west for several kilometres through low-density rural countryside, with the road meandering through narrow valleys until it ended at the base of another small mountainous ridge.

There the Rolls Royce left the road and followed a

narrow track for a further four kilometres along the base of the ridge, before turning in at a run-down, grotty shed that appeared to jut from the side of the rocky cliff. Being the same colour as its stony surroundings, the corrugated iron building was barely visible from afar.

The driver parked the limousine close to the entrance, beside four late model Toyota Landcruisers and an assortment of other vehicles. He wasted no time getting out to open the back door.

A fat man in a suit emerged and leaned in to help another man, shackled around the wrists and ankles, struggle out of the car.

Standing in the afternoon sun, Saddam Akim breathed deeply and threw the fat man a broad grin. He was then taken by the elbow and led around to the back of the vehicle, where one of three guards had taken up position as soon as the limousine arrived.

As they approached the guard tapped on the boot of the Rolls Royce. When it popped open, he leaned in and drew out a large pair of bolt cutters. At the fat man's prompting, Akim put a foot onto the car's rear bumper and the guard swiftly cut his shackles.

With a relieved sigh, he reached down to rub the angry red marks on his ankles and then the procedure was repeated on both his wrists.

Once all his bonds had been removed, Akim embraced the fat man once more, exclaiming in his native tongue, 'Akeem Jibril! My friend, to you I owe my freedom.'

'It is an honour to serve our leader,' Jibril replied, bending his head to hide the calculating gleam in his eyes.

When a guard passed him a bag from the boot he handed it to Akim, saying, 'For you, a change of clothes. You can freshen up inside and change out of those offensive overalls.'

'Yes,' Akim muttered, plucking at his prison garb with harsh fingers. 'The stench of infidel insults my nostrils.'

Limping a little, he followed Jibril inside the shed. It was dimly lit and filled with thick, aromatic smoke from cigarettes, cigars, and burning incense. In contrast to its humble exterior, the building's interior was vast, plush and windowless, giving it a cavernous feel. Its inner walls were whitewashed with a thick mud-clay coating and lined with indoor palms and other leafy plants.

Mesmerising Middle-eastern music droned from concealed speakers throughout the room, and a belly dancer gyrated seductively out of a pocket of darkness, gold bangles and ankle bracelets jingling.

Suspended from the dark-coloured ceilings, decorative glass lanterns cast shadowy multi-coloured light over the floor where large pillows were piled on thick, plush rugs.

A number of partially dressed, bleary-eyed male

patrons were sprawled across the pillows beside opium-laced hookahs, being attended to by dark-skinned and scantily clad young women.

As he was escorted across the main room, Akim peered into the gloom and counted four men with AK47s standing guard, two at the front entrance and two at the rear. Following Jibril into a corridor at the rear of the room, he took in the curtained-off alcoves flanking both sides of its entire length.

As they passed, he heard various carnal sounds coming from within the alcoves, and licked his lips. Jibril noticed his reaction and leered suggestively, pointing ahead.

When the corridor ended in a T junction, they turned right and went through a door into a six-by-six metre, incense and music-filled room. In the centre of the room two young women sat in a spa, naked.

On a ledge beside them an ornate silver hookah had a number of hoses snaking off it. Smiling coquettishly and raising satin-skinned arms, they beckoned him to join them. He needed no further coaxing.

Seeing his leader tear off his prison garb and leap into the bubbling water amid squeals and giggles from the two whores, Jibril's lip curled and he hurriedly turned away.

As he was leaving, he barked at the guard on sentry duty outside the door, 'Make sure all his needs are seen to. I will return later this evening.'

CHAPTER SEVENTEEN

At an altitude of thirty-five thousand feet, the RAAF KC-30A military Airbus roared over Pakistan on its way to Bagram military airfield in Afghanistan.

'We'll be making our descent soon.' Ben unfolded from the seat, rose and stretched.

The others were already awake and did the same, and when he tilted his head toward the rear of the plane, they followed him down there. Opening a laptop, he placed it on the tray in front of the last aisle seat and glanced at the others as they gathered around.

'I've got some intel on the whereabouts of Saddam Akim.'

Four sets of eyes focused on the screen. The NatSec logo twirled in the centre and then a satellite image of Afghanistan appeared.

Modeen glanced at Ben. 'I take it the black ops element of our mission is over now?'

He shook his head. 'Not entirely. Jack Pender was sympathetic when I informed him of my family's abduction and the events of the last few days, and he verbally authorised me to use whatever resources I require to neutralise the threat. But as far as NatSec is concerned,' and he swept them with a significant glance, 'we're all on vacation.'

'We're on holiday?' Spooky thumped him on his broad back. 'Right, let's do some sightseeing.'

With an amused grunt, Ben turned to point at the screen. 'We touch down here at the US military airfield in Bagram. Local time is o-two hundred. The base is approximately sixty kilometres north-east of Kabul. I've arranged to pick up a Bushmaster and supplies.'

'A Bushmaster?' Spooky looked impressed. 'Where'd ya find one of them over here?'

'Australian forces stored some here when they pulled out of Tarin Kowt,' Ben mumbled offhandedly. He paused, contemplating the next sequence of events before saying firmly, 'We'll rendezvous with Bugs in Kabul and head south past lake Hashmat Khan. As of two hours ago Saddam Akim was here,' and he zoomed in on a small structure built into the side of a mountainous ridge. The infra-red image showed a group of thirty vehicles parked outside the building. He tapped on a key. 'This is a thermal image of the structure.'

The screen zoomed in further and the thermal image revealed approximately fifty people in the front room, two people in every alcove on either side of a long rear corridor, and a large heat signature in the centre of the end room off to the right.

Modeen pulled a face at Ben. 'Brothel?'

He nodded and indicated two heat signatures moving on the screen. 'Watch this.'

The two hot spots moved down the length of the corridor and turned left. They continued along a narrow portal for what looked like two hundred metres.

The screen scrolled, following their movements as they left the main building behind and emerged to the west of it, where more heat signatures were gathered.

Ben switched the screen back to infra-red, high-lighting three vehicles parked outside the structure which, from the outside, looked like a smaller version of the main building. A rocky outcrop separated the two buildings and effectively hid the smaller one.

'Our intel suggests that this second building is a meth lab, which is connected to the main building by this portal.'

'Wow,' Wolf muttered darkly, 'we've found ourselves a nice wholesome place here.'

'Yeah,' Spooky nodded, 'a real cesspit.' He turned to Ben. 'So why not just send in a drone and nuke the place? There were two doing nothing back at Bagram.

I'm sure the Yanks wouldn't mind us borrowing one for a bit.'

As though expecting the question Ben replied briskly, 'Except that, judging by its current occupancy, the brothel's doing a roaring trade. If we send in a drone, we can expect a lot of collateral damage. And there might be other innocents being held in there that we don't know about.'

Spooky nodded. 'Point taken.'

'Besides, we need to make sure we gather as much intel as we can, so we don't leave any loose ends.' Ben eyed each of them individually. 'I want to put an end to the *Spear of Allah* once and for all.'

'Excuse me, sir?' An airman came to stand in the aisle in front of them. 'We're starting our descent now, so could you please return to your seats.'

———

Bugs awoke feeling refreshed. He sat up and stretched and checked his watch.

Time for a coffee and a shower.

Yawning, he ambled into the kitchen, plugged in the kettle and glanced over at the sofa. Tony's long frame was sprawled on it and he was snoring gently.

Bugs went over to nudge him with a toe. 'Coffee?'

'What?' Tony jerked awake and sat up, blinking. 'Oh *man.*' He scowled and rubbed his head. 'I was havin' a great dream ... about a blonde—'

Rolling his eyes Bugs said loudly, 'Do you want a coffee?'

'Oh, yeah.' Tony yawned. 'Ta.'

Going over to knock on the spare room door, Bugs called, 'K-man! Time to shake a leg.' Returning to the kitchen, he rinsed out some mugs and set them on the counter. Opening the fridge door, he spotted the carton of UHT milk Karim had opened earlier and took it out.

At the other end of the unit, Karim emerged from the spare bedroom wearing camouflage pants. His hair was tousled and he had a towel draped over one tattooed, muscular shoulder. In a deep, drowsy voice he rumbled, 'Dibs on the first shower.'

'Go for it,' Bugs called. 'We've got plenty of time. We're not meeting Ben and the others for a coupl'a hours.'

'Where're we meetin' them?' Karim paused on his way to the bathroom.

'On the highway heading south.' Bugs poured two coffees and took one to Tony. 'Get that into ya,' he said with a grin.

'Ta, mate.' Taking the mug, Tony gazed at him. 'Say, you know who you look like?'

Raising an eyebrow Bugs said flatly, 'Surprise me.'

'Jake Busey.' When this met with a blank look, Tony explained, 'You know, Jake Busey the actor? The blonde-haired, toothy guy in the movie Starship Troopers? He played the violin.'

Bugs blew him a raspberry, just as Karim's deep

voice boomed from the bathroom doorway. 'Yep, that's who I would've picked you for too. Only you're a bit beefier.'

'Yeah,' Tony said eagerly, 'and I reckon Modeen looks like that Charlize Theron.' He glanced over at Karim, who crinkled his chin thoughtfully and nodded agreement.

Bugs snorted. 'You guys watch *way* too much TV.'

'You can talk,' Tony sniffed. 'Look at the size of that idiot box ya got sittin' in the corner.'

———

Landing lights bordered the three and a half thousand metres of double width runway at the US military base in Bagram as the KC-30A Airbus touched down.

The pilot wasted no time clearing the runway as behind the RAAF plane a C17 Globemaster was preparing for take-off.

The Airbus taxied parallel to the runway past the control tower, support buildings, and the six F-16C Fighting Falcons, three huge US C17 Globemasters, and four US A-10 Thunderbolts parked on the apron.

Two MQ1 Predator drones sat at the entrance to the main US hangar. In comparison to the other aircraft they looked tiny, innocent and unthreatening, proving that looks can be deceiving.

The Airbus came to a halt in front of a hangar with an RAAF emblem in the centre of its tall gable roof.

Floodlights illuminated the large corrugated iron building and cast a glow over five RAAF F/A-18F Super Hornets sitting menacingly on the tarmac to its left.

As the whine of the Airbus' engines wound down to a hum, aluminium stairs were rolled up to the fuselage and the front hatch opened.

Inside, Ben disappeared into the cockpit as Modeen, Wolf and Spooky exited the aircraft, climbing down the stairs and walking across the tarmac into the hangar.

At the back of the massive shed a desert-camouflaged Bushmaster all-terrain vehicle was being checked over by a man in an Australian Army uniform.

He turned on their approach and wiped oily hands on an equally oily rag. 'She's all fuelled up and ready to go.' He frowned. 'My orders were to deck her out for four?'

'Yup.' Wolf jerked a thumb over his shoulder. 'There's one more to come.'

The soldier looked over at the Airbus. Seeing Ben make his way down the stairs and stride purposefully toward them, he nodded. 'Right, follow me. I'll get you kitted out with some camo fatigues and weapons.'

Twenty minutes later they were on the main road from Bagram airfield to Kabul. Ben was behind the wheel of the troop carrier with Modeen beside him. Spooky and Wolf were in the back.

Leaning forward, Spooky raised his voice to be heard over the drone of the seven point two litre, six cylinder turbo-charged engine. 'I'd forgotten how noisy and slow these things are.'

'Yeah,' Wolf growled, 'and they're not comfortable either.' His lips tipped into a crooked grin and he twitched one dark eyebrow. 'But at least they're bulletproof.'

They made their way through Kabul and headed south past Hashmat Khan lake. It was approaching o-four hundred hours when they pulled off the side of the road to rendezvous with Bugs' Humvee. As the Bushmaster rolled to a stop, Bugs, Karim and Tony got out of the Humvee. Climbing into the back of the troop carrier, they pulled the shades over the windows.

Ben climbed out of the front and joined the others in the back, folding his large frame into what little space was left. The vehicle was capable of carrying nine average-sized troopers and a driver comfortably, but with seven occupants, most of them over six foot tall and two of them human leviathans, it felt a little cramped.

Bugs flicked on the overhead light and pointed to his companions. 'Ben, Modeen, Spooky and Wolf, this is Karim and Tony, both from Second Commando Regiment.'

Ben extended a hand in greeting but Tony didn't notice. His eyes were glued on an oblivious Modeen. Shaking Karim's hand instead, Ben gave a knowing grin as Spooky nudged him and whispered, 'The Modeen factor, alive and well.'

Beside Tony, Wolf's eyes glinted. He jabbed an elbow into the other man's ribs, snapping him out of his trance, and growled, 'Listen up.'

Tony glanced around sheepishly and hastened to make good on his greetings, but Ben had already moved on. Placing the laptop on his knee, he brought up a map of the buildings south of the lake.

CHAPTER EIGHTEEN

Ben lifted his chin at Bugs' team. 'Are you guys familiar with the area?'

Tony nodded and Karim said, 'We've flown over it a few times on manoeuvres.'

Ben pointed to the two sheds on the screen. 'We're going to infiltrate these structures. Our specific targets are the SoA leaders ...,' and he tapped on his laptop to bring up four mug shots on the screen, '... Saddam Akim, Akeem Jibril, Abdul Bari, and Jibril's younger brother, Ammil. If we encounter civilians making a run for it we are to let them go, but consider any that take up arms as hostiles.'

Bugs tapped on his tracking app. 'Looks like Akim is still in the main building.'

'From the air,' Karim ventured, 'those sheds look like they're built into the side of the hill, and there's a substantial rocky outcrop between them.'

Ben nodded and ran the satellite thermal imaging footage of the buildings' interiors. 'This was taken over three hours ago, so the crowd may've thinned by now.' When the footage ended, he tapped on the laptop again and brought up a chart of the area's terrain. 'As Karim said, there's a rocky outcrop separating the two buildings, which are approximately two hundred metres apart.' Ben pointed to a spot on the screen. 'I want a sniper positioned here on the other side of the ravine, where there should be a clear view of both entrances.'

Tony rubbed his chin and said doubtfully, 'That looks to be over fifteen hundred metres....'

'Yeah,' Wolf drawled, 'I got this.' Ignoring Tony, he looked at Bugs. 'Did you bring your Lapua Magnum?'

Bugs nodded. 'Even got a coupl'a mags of low drag Wildcats. As you suggested, I've had the chamber and bore modified for 'em.'

Wolf gave a thumbs up as Spooky nudged Modeen and said, 'What, no "Roosters"?'

They both chuckled, but when the others frowned at them questioningly she murmured, 'Long story. We'll tell you later.'

Ben carried on. 'We'll take both vehicles and circle the ravine to where Wolf will take up position. From there we'll proceed on foot. Modeen, Spooky and Tony will make their way down to the meth lab on the western side.' He looked at Modeen. 'Going by the previous footage, you should only come across two armed guards and a few lab workers.'

She nodded and he went on. 'Once you've finished, make your way east along the connecting corridor. Bugs, Karim and I will take the main building. We'll move on my signal.' Digging into his pocket, Ben pulled out a wallet-sized case containing eight comms units. He handed them around, saying, 'Keep in contact and don't put yourselves at undue risk. It'll be dawn in just over an hour, so we only have a small window. Let's get moving.'

Pausing to eyeball Tony and Karim, he said sternly, 'You're new to the team so I want you to listen carefully.'

He waited until he was certain he had their full attention. 'You're seasoned soldiers, you know this mission is important. But not at the expense of any team member.' He fixed them with a steely glance. 'Understood?'

They both nodded and chimed, 'Understood.'

'Good. Now, Modeen I want you to drive. And Bugs, take Karim and Tony in the Humvee. Keep the lights off and use your night vision goggles.'

As the other five piled out of the Bushmaster, Spooky and Wolf stretched out and got comfortable in the back.

Modeen went around the front to climb into the driver's seat and Ben slid into the passenger's side, while the other three jumped into the nearby Humvee.

Firing up the big diesel, Modeen slipped on her night vision goggles and put the Bushmaster into gear. It rumbled into motion as behind them Bugs started the Humvee.

The two vehicles lumbered their way around to the far side of the small valley. Leaving the main track, they bounced along the rocky terrain, taking care to stop about fifty metres back from the edge of the ravine. That kept them out of sight from below. Wolf jumped out of the Bushmaster and went around to Bugs' Humvee. Opening the back, he took out a rectangular aluminium case and assembled the Vanquish .338 Lapua Magnum rifle.

While the others got ready, he placed a spare magazine into the thigh pocket of his cargo pants and checked the weapon, muttering, 'When was the last time you sighted 'er in, Bugs?'

'Just before I left for Oz.' Bugs came to stand beside him. 'That scope's pretty reliable, hasn't given me any problems. She's spot-on at a thousand metres. Here, take these,' and he handed Wolf a pair of camouflage army-issue binoculars and a custom-made silencer for the rifle. 'You can use the binoculars to check the range.'

With a gruff, 'Thanks, mate,' Wolf grabbed a camouflage blanket, walked around the Humvee and disappeared into the darkness.

Getting down on his belly, he crawled the last ten metres to the very edge of the ravine. Lying on his stomach, he raised himself onto his elbows and pulled out the binoculars to check the distances.

1725 metres to the main building's entrance on the east.

1708 to the meth lab entrance on the west.

His current location had him well positioned between the two buildings and gave an elevated view of both. He switched the binoculars to thermal imaging and swept the area, zooming in on a heat signature high on the rocky outcrop between the two buildings.

'How's it look?' Ben had crawled up next to him.

Wolf kept the binoculars to his eyes as he replied softly, 'Sentry on the rocky outcrop between the buildings, about halfway up the ridge.' Lowering the binoculars, he handed them to Ben and turned to screw the custom-made silencer to the barrel of the Vanquish.

After flicking forward the rifle's bipod stand, he made himself comfortable behind the scope.

Seeing Ben lower the binoculars, he murmured, 'Do you want me to take out the sentry?'

Ben didn't answer but put a finger to his comms unit. 'Sound off.'

The responses came back almost immediately.

'Modeen, ready.'

'Spook, ready.'

'Bugs, ready.'

'Karim, ready.'

'Tony, ready.'

Ben checked the distance. 'Target at 1890 metres.' With a thumb and forefinger he took a pinch of dusty soil from the ground in front of him and then held up his hand, sprinkling the dirt from between his fingers. Watching it fall straight back to earth, he muttered, 'Wind negligible.' Putting the binoculars back to his eyes, he focused on the sentry sitting on a rock facing them with an AK47 resting on his lap. 'Whenever you're ready, Wolf.'

Beside him, Wolf's breathing went shallow. The rifle bucked and gave a violent hiss as he let loose a single round. Two and a half seconds later, they watched the sentry crumple and fall backward onto the rocks.

Wolf raised his head. 'Did you see where the bullet hit?'

'Centre of his chest, about an inch and a half to the right.' Ben lowered the binoculars. 'Pretty much straight through the heart.' He waited while Wolf made some fine adjustments to the scope, and in the silence that followed, heard a muttered, 'Ready.'

'Let's move, people,' Ben barked into the comms. 'We need to get across to those buildings before the sun comes up.' Rising to his feet but keeping low, he waited until the others were behind him and then dropped off the edge and led the way down the ravine.

Half way down, Modeen, Spooky and Tony peeled off to the left and navigated through the rocky cliff face. The targets were approximately two hundred metres away on the other side of a dirt track.

Watching their progress through the binoculars,

Wolf spoke quietly into his comms unit. 'Lights in the distance. Two vehicles approaching from the east.'

The teams scrambled up the other side of the ravine and took cover just below the ridge. Two minutes later they saw a couple of battered Toyota pickups approaching, both with two persons seated in the front and two riding shotgun in the back.

The vehicles came to a halt in front of the brothel and their occupants stowed their weapons. They alighted and moved toward the building, their silhouettes briefly illuminated by the light as they opened the entrance door and stepped inside.

Wolf pressed his comms. 'Just more clients arriving, comin' off night shift.'

Bugs cut in, 'The Rolls Royce that picked up Akim isn't here, but the tracking device tells me he's dead in front of us, about a hundred and fifty metres away.'

Hearing that, Ben commanded, 'Move in.'

Both teams broke cover and, keeping low, raced across the open space to the other side of the dirt track, where they took cover among the vehicles parked in front of the sheds. Slinging his M4 Carbine, Bugs followed Ben. Crossing his arms as he ran, he pulled two jet black fifty calibre Desert Eagle pistols from his shoulder holsters.

Karim stayed close covering their six, MP5 at the ready. When Ben took cover behind one of the Toyota pickups that had just pulled in, Bugs and Karim did the same to the pickup on his right. From his position Ben heard the sound of a motor running close by.

A gen set.

He took a quick glance toward the sound and said over the comms, 'Hold positions.' Running over to a small wooden shelter near the base of the large rocky outcrop between the two sheds, he knelt to study the generator for a second, and then turned off the fuel line.

Racing back to the pickup, he was breathing hard when he spoke into the comms. 'I've just shut off the fuel to their generator. Be ready with your night vision goggles. We'll go on my mark.'

Modeen, Spooky and Tony had positioned them-selves behind the vehicles parked near the meth lab's entrance. Slinging her MP5, Modeen took the Glock from her shoulder holster, pulled back and released the slide. Turning to Tony, she whispered, 'Spooky and I will lead while you cover our six.'

He nodded his understanding.

The lab's interior lights glowed from the narrow gap beneath the entrance door. The glow began to pulse in rhythm with the diesel generator as it surged and spluttered. The motor gave one last cough and the lights inside both sheds went out.

And over the comms, Ben gave the command.

'Go!'

CHAPTER NINETEEN

Modeen kept low as she opened the door to the lab. Leading with her Glock, she darted inside. Spooky was close behind her and as she went left, he went right. Tony remained crouched near the entrance, covering them with his MP4. All three wore night vision goggles and could see clearly in the gloom.

The building's occupants, the lab technicians and guards, stood murmuring and making disgruntled rumblings about the power outage. The only light in the room emitted from the gas burners heating beakers on the central lab table. The glow illuminated the immediate area enough to cast eerie shadows around the room.

Spooky and Modeen kept to the shadowy edges, using the hundreds of chemical and solvent boxes stacked in high rows for cover, drawing ever nearer the two guards at the rear of the room.

Within metres of the guards, they positioned themselves in the corners of the lab, paused and aimed. But before they could fire their weapons, Tony released two short bursts from his MP4 from the lab's entrance.

As bursts of light and deafening noise erupted in the room, the guards slumped to the floor. Standing close to the walls, Modeen and Spooky were showered with dust and shards of rock and clay.

Coughing violently, Modeen stepped forward and was momentarily blinded when the emergency lights flicked on. She pulled down her night vision goggles just in time to see one of the lab technicians pick up an AK47.

Multiple shots rang out amid the din.

The technician collapsed to the floor, shot in the head by Modeen and through the neck by Spooky. Out of the corner of her eye, Modeen saw Tony sink to his knees at the entrance and fall backward into the dust.

The remaining lab technicians scarpered out the door as Spooky and Modeen raced over to kneel beside Tony's prone, unmoving form.

They grabbed his vest and dragged him toward the wall, leaving behind a wet red trail on the floor.

When they propped his upper body against the wall, his head slumped forward and then sideways. They squatted beside him and Spooky inspected his wounds, rasping through clenched teeth, 'Find something to pack these with.'

As she jumped to her feet Modeen glimpsed his hands.

They were crimson with blood.

In her hurried search, she found a box of clean rags. Grabbing a handful, she rushed back and handed them to Spooky.

Focused intently on his task, he took them from her without speaking. Folding them roughly he pushed them beneath Tony's vest and pressed them against the wounds, applying pressure to staunch the bleeding.

Outside they heard vehicles starting up and roaring away into the distance.

At the same time as Modeen and Spooky entered the meth lab, on the other side of the outcrop Ben had run up and kicked in the main building's entrance door. He took two long strides into the room with Bugs right behind him.

While Ben levelled his MP5 and took out the two guards at the rear of the room, Bugs spread his arms wide and neutralised the guards on either side of the entrance door.

Mayhem erupted inside the brothel as men, clutching their clothes, scurried from the corridor's alcoves. In the main room, some scrambled for the exit. Others, too drugged to move, watched the proceedings through bleary, unfocused eyes. Partly dressed women wailed and screamed and cowered in the darkness.

Two men bounced off Karim as he entered the main room. Stumbling to their feet, they squeezed past him in the darkness and escaped the building. Taking up position at the entrance, Karim stood fast while Ben and Bugs started toward the rear corridor. They were temporarily blinded as the emergency lights came on, and quickly yanked down their night vision goggles.

Karim shaded his eyes and was immediately set upon by two of the larger males. Their advancing punches had little effect on the big man. He grabbed one by the throat and the top of his pants and went to throw him outside. The man smashed head-first into the wall to the left of the front entrance and fell motionless in a heap.

Karim's aim was better with the second man, who sailed through the doorway to land heavily in the dirt three metres outside the front door.

A third man pulled a machete from underneath a stack of floor pillows. Holding it high, he gave a blood-curdling yell and ran at Karim.

From across the room, a deafening blast from one of Bugs' Desert Eagles silenced the man abruptly. His legs collapsed from under him and he careered to the floor. The other male patrons gave Karim a wide berth as they rushed toward the exit.

• • •

Up on the ridge, Wolf watched as the two lab technicians sped past in a late model Toyota Landcruiser. He trained his high-powered rifle scope on the door of the brothel and watched two men scamper outside into the pale light of the dawn. They ran to one of the battered pickups and each took out an AK47 assault rifle.

Thrusting his rifle into the air in a show of bravado, the first man turned to run back into the brothel, but only took a few steps before falling face-first into the dirt.

Seeing that, the other man spun around and took refuge behind the front of the vehicle. His head was just visible above the bonnet as he pointed his weapon aimlessly up at the ridge, straining to see who had fired at them. Seconds later the back of his head exploded and his lifeless body sagged backward.

Seeing another man flying through the air from out of the front door, arms and legs flailing uselessly, Wolf gave an amused grunt.

When the man hit the ground heavily from a height of about five feet, the impact brought up a plume of dust. He lay still for a couple of seconds and then staggered to his feet and made his way to the battered pickup.

Wolf continued watching as the man bent to collect the AK47 lying beside one of his dead companions. Staggering to the back of the pickup, he swung himself up behind the cab. The moment he rested the weapon on the roof and trained it at the front door, he was a dead man. Within seconds his body had given a violent jerk before collapsing and sliding off the side of the ute and onto the ground.

Wolf's focus returned to the building's front entrance as a stampede of people jostled in their panic to get out. He scanned their faces, looking for any resemblance to the mug shots Ben had shown them earlier.

Inside, Ben and Bugs advanced down the corridor, leaving Karim in the now empty main room. Slinging his Carbine, Ben led with his Glock. As they made their way down the corridor, they flicked aside the curtains on the alcoves, checking they were empty. When Ben flicked back the curtain on the last alcove he stiffened. Turning so his huge frame filled the opening, he stared into the tiny room.

Saddam Akim lay sprawled on a mass of pillows, his lower body partly covered by a silk sheet. His skinny arms, coated in thick curls of jet black hair, were flung over the two naked prostitutes curled against his scrawny body. One of the women raised her head to look at Ben. She squinted and blinked, her pupils unnaturally dilated.

When Akim began to stir, Ben finally spoke. 'Do you know who I am?' he growled. When he raised his Glock, the two prostitutes roused themselves and shuffled away from Akim to cower in the corners of the alcove.

Sitting up to blink groggily at Ben, Akim spat in a

thick accent, 'What does it matter who *you* are? *I* am the Spear of Allah. You are nothing, just another stinking infidel.'

'Yeah, you're right, it doesn't matter.' Ben aimed the Glock. 'And a spear without a head is just a stick.' Amid shrieks from the two women, he pulled the trigger. Akim's head rocked back and his arms and leg splayed as his body sagged into the plush pillows beneath him.

Bugs had slipped past Ben to check the spa room to the right. He found it empty. Ben met him at the end of the hallway just as Modeen hurried toward them from the connecting corridor on their left.

'Tony's been hit,' she said grimly into her comms unit. 'Right shoulder and lower left abdomen.'

Wolf's voice crackled over the comms. 'We've got a Blackhawk coming in from the north-east, one of ours.' He was watching it thunder around the mountain ridge past Beni Hisar.

Ben pressed a finger to his comms piece. 'Karim, try to get their attention. We'll need to evac Tony.'

Karim barked, 'Roger,' as he turned on his heel and sprinted out the main building's front entrance. Once outside, he shaded his eyes from the morning light and took a survey of the area. All but one of the vehicles had gone.

Seeing the three bodies beside the old pickup, he looked up at the ridge. After throwing a quick salute in Wolf's direction, he located the low-flying helicopter and began waving his arms in the air, trying to attract their attention.

Bugs tapped Ben on the arm. 'There's a two-way radio in my Humvee. Wolf could make contact with the chopper if they miss Karim.'

Ben rapped over the comms, 'Wolf, there's a two-way in the Humvee. Get the chopper to land in front of the meth lab. JD, go back and help Spooky with Tony. Bugs and I will do a sweep of the building and meet you at the front of the lab.'

Wolf was about to get up when a trail of dust off to the west caught his eye. Using Bugs' binoculars, he saw an old Toyota Landcruiser pull up just at the crest of the ridge. The roof of the wagon had been cut off and he could see a rebel standing on the passenger's seat loading an RPG.

The helicopter was coming in low, unaware of the threat that lay ahead, homing in on Karim standing out in the open waving his arms above his head. Taking note of the range, Wolf swung the sniper rifle around, calculating the necessary ballistic adjustments on the fly.

Eighteen hundred and fifty metres.

The rebel with the RPG heaved it onto the top of the windscreen. He aimed the weapon at the incoming helicopter, preparing to fire, but then sat back heavily into the rear seat. The driver frowned and glanced around to see the rebel's bloodied head fall to the side and his body follow it to the floor.

Starting the car, the driver swung it around in a shower of gravel and sped off, just as Wolf let loose another round. The vehicle's windscreen splattered red and the Toyota wobbled, veering off the edge of the dirt track, before careering down the side of the ridge.

Unaware of the drama unfolding close by, the helicopter had descended to within metres of Karim, who indicated for the pilot to go to the other side of the rocky outcrop. He obliged, and the big machine powered up and over to the other side.

Spooky and Modeen had dragged Tony outside into the open. At the Blackhawk's approach, they turned their backs to it and sheltered their injured team mate from the storm of dust kicked up by the choppers' blades.

A medic sprang from the Blackhawk as it touched down and raced over to them. 'What the hell are you guys doing out here?' he yelled over the roar of the helicopter's engines.

Indicating Tony, Spooky yelled back, 'He's been shot in the shoulder and abdomen and is losing blood fast. I've given him a jab of morphine but he needs urgent medical attention.'

'Right.' The medic focused on the injured man. 'Let's get him on the chopper.'

Modeen took Tony's feet as Spooky and the medic grabbed a handful each of his vest and lifted him onto the Blackhawk's platform.

When they backed away, the medic shouted, 'You coming with us?'

'No.' Spooky shook his head. 'We'll catch up with you later.'

Keeping their heads low, they watched the chopper rise into the air. The pilot swung it wide and followed the ravine west, before circling back toward Kabul and Bagram airbase. He banked sharply to the north just as a vehicle exploded below them. Not bothering to investigate the explosion, the pilot opened the throttle and thundered back to base.

Modeen and Spooky went back to the lab where they met Ben and Bugs.

'How badly was Tony hurt?' Ben rapped.

When Spooky replied, 'The bullet in his shoulder isn't too bad,' Modeen found her fingers feeling the scar on her own shoulder, and winced. 'It missed his lungs,' he continued, 'but the wound in his abdomen looks nasty. He was losing a lot of blood. I'd say he might come out of it minus a kidney and/or his spleen.'

Ben shook his head gravely. 'What happened?'

Modeen stepped forward. 'His orders were to guard our six as we entered the building, but for some reason he opened fire from the entranceway. Spooky and I were showered with fragments of wall and dust, and then the emergency lights came on and blinded us for a couple of seconds. That was enough time for this lab technician,' and she nudged a body on the floor with her boot, 'to get off a couple of shots before we could stop him.'

'They're too used to working on their own.' Karim strode into the room from the connecting corridor. 'Snipers typically don't play well with others, 'tho Wolf appears to be an exception.'

'Well, let's hope Tony pulls through,' Ben said, his tone becoming businesslike again. 'Now, there's not a lot of intel here, but this order form might give us a lead.' He held it up. 'Three hundred boxes are going to whoever this is,' and he pointed to a red banner with Arabic wording on it beneath what appeared to be an ornate, gilded spearhead. 'And even more interestingly, two thousand boxes were meant to be consigned to one I Singh with an Aussie email address. I'll get the Arabic wording interpreted back at the base.'

Taking the order form from him, Karim peered at the banner. 'Hey Bugs, check this out. Does this look familiar to you?'

Bugs looked over his shoulder and muttered, 'It sure does.'

Karim glanced at Ben. 'No need for an interpretation, we know where this is.' He handed back the form. 'It's not that far from the Embassy.'

'Right.' Ben slipped the order into his top pocket. 'We'll head back across the ravine and rendezvous at Bagram base, to check on Tony and grab a quick breakfast. Spooky, Modeen.' He inclined his head to indicate the room. 'You know what to do.'

They made their way out of the lab, and as Ben, Bugs and Karim jogged toward the ravine, Modeen and Spooky yanked two grenades from the front of their webbing.

Locking eyes with Spooky, Modeen counted down, 'Three ... two ... one.'

They pulled the pins and hurled the grenades into the lab before turning to sprint after the others. Behind them, the combination of grenade blasts and volatile chemicals in the lab produced a spectacular fiery backdrop to their departure.

CHAPTER TWENTY

Wolf monitored the progress of the five as they came back across the ravine. When they were within fifty metres of him he broke cover and rose to his feet. Draping the camouflage blanket over a burly shoulder, he picked up the Vanquish sniper rifle, pulled back the bolt and cleared the chamber.

Ben was the first to appear at the top of the ridge. He glanced to the west at a thin pillar of black smoke and raised an eyebrow at Wolf. Clapping him on the shoulder as he passed, he said with a half smile, 'You can tell me about that over breakfast.'

The next over the ridge was Karim. Wolf turned to him and frowned. 'What happened to Tony?'

Dragging a hand over his face, Karim muttered tightly, 'He took one in the shoulder and one in the gut.'

'What calibre?'

'Seven point six two, from an AK47.'

Wolf winced. 'Hope he pulls through.'

'Me too.' Karim trudged on but paused to throw over his shoulder, 'Nice shootin', by the way.'

When the other three arrived at the top of the ravine they caught up with Wolf and Karim, and as a group followed Ben back to the vehicles. They moved quietly without speaking, heads lowered, their thoughts with their injured comrade.

In the Humvee, Bugs stared fixedly through the windscreen as he followed the Bushmaster back to Bagram airbase. They parked at the RAAF hangar and immediately headed to the base's giant military medical centre, where they knew Tony would have been taken.

When he stepped up to the reception counter, Ben was told by the young female officer on duty that Tony was in the operating theatre. Giving Ben a significant glance, she added that they expected him to be in there for a while.

Ben gave a tight-lipped nod. 'Could you text me when he's able to have visitors?'

She handed him a Post-it note, her eyes sympathetic as she gazed into his worried, dust-smudged face.

After scrawling his mobile number on the note and handing it back to her, he turned to his team. 'We'll grab a quick breakfast and debrief, then we need to keep moving.'

Bugs led the way to the mess, where they lined up and took a tray each, still without speaking.

A sudden cheery voice shook them out of their apprehensive glumness. 'Hey, Bugsy!' The American voice came from near one of the bain-maries. 'Whatcha doin' here, boy? I thought you were going to be in Oz for a couple of months?'

Looking over to see a grinning US private dressed in food-splattered white chef's gear, Bugs called, 'Had to come back early. Was missin' your great tucker.'

The private gave an amused snort. 'As if!'

Bugs sauntered over to him. 'Hey, speaking of tucker, you guys ever thought about includin' seafood chowder on the menu?' He raised hopeful eyebrows, but the private merely guffawed and blew him a raspberry.

'What, ya puttin' in orders now? This ain't a cordon bleu establishment, y'know!'

Bugs grinned. 'Just a suggestion.' He shrugged and walked away.

Ben's team sat at the end of a long row of tables, emptying their plates quietly and quickly.

Pushing the despised powdered egg omelette to the side of her otherwise clean plate, Modeen joined Spooky and Wolf at the urn and refilled her coffee cup.

When they returned to the table, Ben leaned in and lowered his voice as he went over the morning's events.

Taking the order form out of his pocket, he placed it in the centre of the table. 'We need to check out this lead, ASAP. News of our little raid this morning will've travelled fast.' He tapped the top of the form with a finger and eyed Karim and Bugs. 'What can you tell us about the red banner?'

Bugs' cheeks bulged with the last of his bacon, eggs and toast breakfast so Karim answered for them both. 'We've seen it on a building near the embassy.'

'Location and type of building?'

'It's an older style place, mud and clay construction with two storeys. Those kinds of places typically have a shopfront or storage area on the bottom level and offices or residences above.' Karim frowned, recalling. 'I'm pretty sure this one is in the middle of a row of similar buildings.'

Bugs swallowed and spoke up. 'The buildings on the street behind are mirror images of the ones in the front. They back onto them and share common walls. The shops have a basic front door and the only parking's out on the street. Most of the places have been modernised a bit. Things like aluminium-framed windows and single roller doors facin' the street, for loadin' stock 'n stuff.'

Ben gave a brisk nod. 'Sounds like the only way to come at them is from the front.' He swept a glance around the table. 'We can assume the hostiles have either bugged out, or have dug in and will be ready for us.'

Setting down his coffee mug and brushing crumbs from his hands, he said crisply, 'We'll take both vehicles and park down the street from the location. Depending on the available vantage points, I want sniper cover.'

He rose to his feet. 'We'll sort out the details when we get there. Any questions?'

When nobody spoke, he barked, 'Right, let's move out.'

———

Akeem Jibril took a drag on his stogie and, savouring it, leaned back behind his double pedestal desk. Narrowing his eyes, he stared through the smoke at his second in command.

Abdul Bari stood before the imposing desk shuffling his feet and flicking worried glances around the room.

Swallowing, he said with a tremor in his voice, 'Our operations to the south were raided this morning.' He cleared his throat and continued. 'Our leader has been assassinated.'

Jibril's lips twisted and he flicked a hand dismissively. 'It matters not about Akim. The man was a fool, allowing himself to be caught and incarcerated by the infidels. He put the whole operation at risk.' He leaned back in his chair.

Bari stammered, 'B-but he was—'and earned himself a dark glance from Jibril, who sat forward and took the stogie from his mouth.

Fixing Bari with a penetrating glance, he kept his voice low and threatening. '*I* am the leader now, the spearhead of Allah. At last *I* am in control, and you will follow *my* orders.'

'Of c-course.' Wringing his hands, Bari gave a vigorous nod of his head and tried to smile but only managed to look pained.

Jibril put the cigar in his mouth again, took a long drag, and sat back to blow the smoke into the air above Bari. 'They will not stop there, these infidels,' he said contemplatively, 'but we will be ready for them. Go! Bring Ammil to me. We have some preparations to make.' And he dismissed Bari with a wave of his bejewelled hand.

———

It was o-eight thirty Kabul time when a Bushmaster turned into the street, followed closely by a desert-camouflaged Humvee.

Karim stiffened in the passenger's seat and muttered, 'Pull over here.'

Ben promptly braked and nosed the Bushmaster onto the verge as Karim lifted his chin to indicate the right side of the street. 'It's that middle building. See the red banner above the front door?'

Ben eyed the building, noting the jostle of passing pedestrians going about their business. But compared to other streets in Kabul, this one was relatively quiet. He put a finger to his comms unit. 'Five hundred metres down on the right, middle building, red banner above the door.'

From the front seat of the Humvee, Bugs and Wolf craned their necks to gaze at the buildings on the other side of the road, taking special note of their rooflines.

'There,' Wolf said sharply, 'that crappy block of flats with a water tank on the roof. It's got a service ladder to the tank from the outside.'

As Wolf made to get out of the vehicle, Bugs tapped him on the shoulder and said, 'I think I can handle this one?'

Wolf paused to stare at him thoughtfully, and nodded.

Putting a finger to his comms, Bugs announced, 'I've got the entrance covered from the roof on the left.' As he spoke, he got out of the Humvee and went around to the back to take out the case containing the sniper rifle.

Sliding it into a custom-made back pack, and slipping a spare magazine of .338 Wildcats and the silencer into the pockets of his cargo pants, he slung the pack over his shoulder and set off toward the block of flats.

Wolf watched him stroll down the street casually

weaving in and out of the pedestrians, and then his strawberry-blonde flat-top disappeared as he slipped into a narrow alleyway. Sliding across the bench seat, Wolf got behind the wheel and kept his eyes fixed on the block of flats. A moment later he saw Bugs swiftly ascend the narrow metal stairs leading to the roof.

Leaping off the stairs at the top, Bugs kept low as he ran to the far end of the building. Taking cover behind a metre high façade, he got down on one knee and assembled the rifle. A short time later he said over the comms, 'Bugs in position.'

Straightaway Ben commanded, 'Wolf, go around the block and park at the other end of the street.'

Wolf started the Humvee and did a tight U-turn before accelerating down the road.

In the Bushmaster, Ben turned to Karim. 'I want you to stay here, in case we need extra backup from ground level or a quick getaway.' At Karim's nod, Ben turned to peer at the others in the back of the vehicle. 'Spooky, JD, you're with me. Pistols only for this one, we don't want to scare the locals if we can help it.' Emerging from the back of the Bushmaster, Modeen and Spooky joined Ben on the verge.

He took the lead as they strode down the street toward the target building, but bent as though to tie a shoelace when Bugs' voice erupted from their comms units. 'Stand fast!' He was peering at the target building through the scope of the sniper rifle. The bottom three quarters of the front window had been frosted out, but from his vantage point he could see through the clear glass in the top section. 'I've got two hostiles, bottom room, back corner, roller door end. Armed with assault rifles trained on the front door.'

Ben looked up to see the Humvee appear at the top of the street.

Over the rumble of the big diesel engine Wolf yelled, 'I've got this!' and punched the Humvee through the gears. Charging down the street toward the building, he went as wide as he could until he was parallel to the roller door, where he spun the wheel hard.

With a howl of its all-terrain tyres, the big 4WD bounced up the verge as he threw it down a gear, pushed his boot to the floor, and drove it straight at the roller door.

Inside the building, the two hostiles were positioned behind a stack of cartons. They snapped their heads sideways at the roar of the charging Humvee's motor, followed by the deafening metallic crunch when it slammed into the roller door which was sent careering toward them. The bulky vehicle kept coming, shoving the door before it and compressing the boxes.

The men shrieked and scrambled back only to be pinned against the wall when the Humvee finally came to a stop.

By that time, Ben and the others were at the building. When Ben threw his weight against the shop's front door and shouldered it open, he toppled into the room with Modeen hot on his heels, Glock at the ready.

Inside two more armed hostiles had been moving toward the Humvee with their weapons trained on it. They gave startled yells when Ben and Modeen burst into the room behind them and made to shift their aim to the new intruders. Moving swiftly, Modeen locked her pistol against the barrel of the closest man's rifle, shoving it away.

Grabbing the front of his robes, she kneed him in the groin, lifting him off the ground with the powerful blow. As he fell gasping and whimpering to his knees, she glimpsed the Gurkha Kukri in a scabbard strapped to his chest. In a swift movement, she yanked out the thick, curved blade.

Pivoting backwards on her right leg and using a smooth back-handed movement, she drove the Kukri deep into the second man's throat. As he dropped his weapon and crumpled to the floor gurgling, she reefed out the bloody blade and pivoted smoothly back to plunge the knife hard into the first man's neck.

Nearby, Ben had regained his balance after rushing the door. Raising his Glock, he let loose two quick rounds and silenced the two wailing men still pinned by the roller door. Then he marched up the stairs to the second level, closely followed by Spooky and Modeen.

In the Humvee, Wolf had spied the armed men approaching and had taken cover, bending low across the front seat. Once the sounds of fighting and gunfire had stopped, he lifted his head and looked around.

Seeing all was clear, he got out and straightaway jumped behind the counter to check the rear of the premises.

Making his way down a narrow passage, he came to two closed doors on the left. He walked past the first and stopped. Reaching behind, he flung the door open.

When nothing moved in the room he poked his head around the doorjamb and saw a naked blonde woman lying in the foetal position on a stained mattress. She was cuffed to the iron bed frame, and when he approached she turned her head to gaze up at him through wide, dilated pupils. On the pale, delicate skin of both her inner arms he saw fresh needle marks and dark bruising.

Frowning, he pulled back and went to check the next room. It too contained a blonde woman, also handcuffed and in the same physical condition. But this one was moaning and clutching a filthy sheet to her as though trying to cover her nakedness. Tears ran down her badly scratched and dirty face.

Hearing a squeal of tyres outside the building, Wolf sprinted back down the corridor and vaulted over the counter. He arrived at the smashed shopfront in time to see the Bushmaster slam head-on into a Rolls Royce on the street in front of the shop. As he watched, a door opened on the Roller and an armed man leapt out but didn't make it past the door before falling to the ground, blood streaming from the base of his neck.

A second man crouched behind the open driver's side door, but before he could level his rifle at the Bushmaster his head snapped back and he slumped to the road. The remaining two men in the back seat of the vehicle kicked open the doors and tried to make a run for either side of the verge. Wolf took cover at the side of the doorway, but needn't have bothered. Bugs put a bullet in the insurgent running to the right, and was aiming at the other when Karim leapt from the Bushmaster and sent the man to the asphalt with a single round from his MP4.

Stepping into the open, Wolf signalled for Karim to join him, and the big man jogged over to his side.

CHAPTER TWENTY-ONE

There was a brooding feeling inside the building, a deceptive stillness. On the second level, Ben strode past a single closed doorway positioned to the left of the passageway. Raising a hand at Modeen and Spooky behind him, he gestured for them to move back. Reaching back, he flung open the door and cautiously poked his head around the doorjamb. But he jerked it back again as a deafening blast from a twelve gauge shotgun sent dust and shards of clay flying from the wall behind him.

He barked, 'Give it up, Jibril.'

This met with harsh laughter and a taunt. 'Come in and we'll talk about it.'

Ben lifted his chin toward Spooky, who pulled a grenade from his vest and threw it to him before joining Modeen in backing down the passageway.

'Last chance, Jibril,' Ben called. 'Give up now if you want to live.'

After another burst of manic laughter, Jibril shouted, 'You infidels! You think you can come here and tell me what to do in my own country?'

'Have it your way,' Ben pulled the pin from the grenade and tossed it into the room before backing to the end of the passageway.

Jibril's plush office exploded.

As the dust and debris began to settle, Ben made his way back to the shattered room.

Dust hung thickly in the air. All the same, he could see Jibril's bloodied body slumped over what had been an ornate wooden desk but which was now broken in half and riddled with shrapnel. A large hutch had fallen against his blast-battered body, crushing and pinning it.

As Ben turned to leave, a man cowering behind a plush armchair next to the door rose with a bellow and charged at him with a raised machete in his hand. Whipping around to face his attacker, Ben raised a leg and stomped him squarely in the chest. The man staggered back and as he hit the armchair heavily, Ben aimed his Glock and fired.

Behind him, Modeen and Spooky slipped into the room. Seeing them, Ben pointed to the armchair. 'Abdul Bari.' Then he indicated the desk. 'Akeem Jibril.'

Bugs' voice crackled over the comms. 'We need to make tracks, the local law's heading this way.'

Modeen and Spooky raced out of the room and sprinted down the stairs, taking them two at a time, to find Wolf back behind the wheel of the Humvee. They saw Karim standing at the gaping hole in the shopfront, waving them outside and into the Bushmaster.

As all three of them leapt aboard, Karim started the hulking vehicle and threw it into gear, promptly ramming it into the Rolls Royce and clearing a way for the Humvee to back out.

Inside, Ben came running down the stairs carrying a handful of ledgers and papers. He jumped into the passenger's side of the Humvee as Wolf threw it into reverse and planted his foot.

The tyres squealed and smoked as the big 4WD emerged from the building. Swinging it hard onto the road, Wolf chucked it into first gear and roared off with the Bushmaster close behind. He braked hard in front of the block of flats as Bugs ran out to dive into the back seat, and then planted his foot again.

'Hey,' Bugs exclaimed, 'who've we got here?'

Whipping his head around Ben peered over the seat to see two blonde women wrapped in blankets, heads resting on their crossed arms on the seat and their lower halves on the floor. Both had a handcuff around one slender wrist.

'I found them in the back room,' Wolf barked,

working the gears and pushing the Humvee hard. 'They were chained to beds. Karim helped me free them and carry them out and pile them in here. I think they're American.'

Ben frowned at him. 'How can you tell?'

Wolf gave a snort. 'We were puttin' them in the back seat and one of 'em said,' and he put on his best Southern American accent, "Ya'll be careful now".'

'Hey!' Bugs exclaimed, 'they're probably the two journalists Braden told us about. We'd better take 'em to Eggers base,' he added thoughtfully, 'he'll know who to contact about 'em, and what to do.'

While Major Cody Braden was full of praise for the return of the two journalists, he was indifferent to the non-return of Saddam Akim. He shook Ben's hand vigorously and did the same to Wolf and Bugs.

'I know once they're coherent enough, those lil' ladies will wanna thank you personally,' he enthused, 'but as soon as they're physically able to travel, they're gonna be flown to the States, back to the waitin' arms of their grateful families.'

'Glad we could help.' Ben gave a brusque nod. 'I'll pass on your thanks to the rest of our team.'

They left Eggers barracks shortly afterward to rendezvous with the others at Bagram airbase. A solemn-faced Modeen was waiting for them as they pulled up at the RAAF hangar.

She walked out to greet them, shoulders slumped and hands shoved deep in the pockets of her pants.

Stopping in front of Ben she looked up at him and said sadly, 'Tony didn't make it.'

Ben exhaled and hung his head, while Bugs stared despondently at her and Wolf moved closer to put a comforting hand on her arm. She blinked and gazed up at him.

After a long silence Bugs said quietly, 'How is Karim takin' it?'

Pressing her lips together she gave a slight shake of her head. 'Pretty hard. He blames himself for Tony being on the mission in the first place.'

'I'll have a word with him.' Ben raised his head as he spoke. 'Tony will get the recognition and military burial he deserves.'

Nothing more was said until finally Ben gave a deep sigh.

'I've arranged for us to bunk here tonight and catch another KC30-A heading back to Oz tomorrow, leaving at o-nine hundred. But for now, we can return the gear and then wind down. I need to report to the base commander but I'll catch up with you and we'll have a debrief over lunch in the mess.' With that, he turned and strode out of the hangar.

The team was already tucking into their meals when Ben joined them in the mess hall. They had left an empty spot for him at the head of their table, and he seated himself without speaking and started into his meal.

The others finished before him, but merely pushed their empty plates to the side and sat back to wait patiently.

Setting down his cutlery and wiping his hands, he announced, 'There were a couple of container IDs and consignment notes in the ledgers and documents I retrieved from Jibril's office that made interesting reading, especially the bits about Ivan Singh's import activities, of which I've informed Wyatt and Craig. That information should help them wrap things up and put Singh away for a long time. It appears he was using his political status to get the containers of drugs and weapons fast-tracked through customs.'

Pausing, he took a sip of coffee before continuing. 'And I can confirm that three of the major targets have been neutralised – Akim, Bari and Jibril.'

'Jibril's younger brother was drivin' the Roller,' Bugs piped up. 'I got a good look at him through my scope, so that makes the four.'

'I can confirm that too,' Karim interjected. 'I saw him up close through the windscreen of the Bush-master when I was customising the front end of the Roller.'

'So, all four major targets were neutralised, and we received high praise from the US military for the return of the two journalists.' Ben nodded his appreciation at them all. 'Well done team.' Rising, he leaned across the table to shake Karim's hand. 'And thanks for helping us out at such short notice, mate. If you're at a loose end after you get out of the force, look me up. We can always use a good man like you.'

'Thanks, sir, glad I could help,' the big man mumbled, looking self-conscious but also pleased.

Ben sat back and addressed them all. 'And I'd like to personally thank you all again for the safe rescue of my family. They wouldn't be alive today if not for your expertise, dedication and creative thinking.'

'We just followed your trail of breadcrumbs,' Modeen chuckled.

'Yeah,' Spooky laughed, 'and Modeen's radar.'

'Hear, hear,' the others chanted.

'Well, I'm thankful and proud of you all.' Ben's smiling face grew serious. 'And let's hope we've put a stop to this terrorist group.' Looking at Bugs, he asked, 'You coming back to finish your stint in Oz?'

'Heck yeah! I've got appointments with my son and the half-assembled GT Shaker in a shed in Adelaide. So if Karim's OK to look after my pad while I'm gone ...?'

Bugs glanced at his buddy who nodded his agreement, muttering, 'Long as you don't mind me cleanin' up the place a bit.'

'Right,' Ben said, 'we're leaving here at o-nine hundred tomorrow.'

Outside the windows of the café, Melbourne's inner city was bustling, as usual. Ben and his team sat at a booth at the rear of the well-patronised establishment, chatting and laughing together while waiting for their orders to arrive.

Shouting his team lunch before they left to return home had been a spur of the moment decision for Ben, who gazed around the table with a benevolent expression.

Opposite him Spooky sat in the corner next to Wolf, who looked unusually relaxed with both arms resting casually along the back of the booth. Beside him, Modeen sat at the end of the bench seat. And beside Ben, Bugs sat chuckling at Spooky's jokes and flashing his trademark toothy grin.

Nearby, one of the waitresses turned up the volume on a wall-mounted television to hear a reporter outline breaking news stories. At the reporter's first words, Ben and his team stopped talking and pricked their ears.

'Capital Hill today welcomed the safe return of Harrison Baker, the forthcoming Ambassador to Afghanistan.'

The camera panned to the scene outside Parliament House, where Harrison Baker stood with his wife and children at his sides.

Smiling into the camera, Baker declared, 'I'd like to thank everyone involved in my rescue, and particularly the special forces operatives to whom I owe my life.' He pulled his wife and children in close. 'It's great to back with my family.' Turning with his arms around them, he walked up the stairs of Parliament House.

The camera zoomed in to follow their progress, highlighting the neat white dressing on the back of Baker's head.

Modeen nudged Spooky in the ribs. 'That was a nice job you did on him,' and they all laughed.

The reporter continued speaking. 'Ivan Singh, understudy to Ambassador Baker, has been arrested on charges of importing banned substances and conspiring with terrorists. It is not yet known whether the two cases are related.'

The mug shots of two blonde journalists flashed onto the screen.

'In another turn of events,' the reporter went on, 'two US journalists, Sally Cockburn and Sharon Harris, have been returned safely to their families in the States. It is believed they were rescued by US Marines who raided a terrorist stronghold in Kabul.'

'Humph!' Wolf grunted sourly. 'Well isn't that just typical.'

'Yeah,' Ben said begrudgingly, 'but remember, we weren't supposed to be there. And on the bright side, the commander of Bagram base gave me some great footage, knowing we wouldn't share it. It shows a sniper taking out a rebel who was lining up to fire an RPG-7 at a Blackhawk. It seems they had a drone overhead on routine surveillance at the time.' He reached over to thump Wolf on the arm. 'Nice shooting, by the way.'

'Yeah, great gun too, eh Wolf?' Bugs said proudly. 'Hey, you didn't say what you thought of the mods to the Lapua?'

'She'll do.' Wolf threw him a wink.

A waitress arrived and distributed their meals.

'It's a shame Emily couldn't make it,' Modeen said. 'Isn't this her favourite café?'

'Yeah, but she was quite happy to sit this one out, reckons she's had enough excitement for a while,' Ben said wryly. 'And besides, I'm going to keep them at the safehouse for a bit longer, 'til the dust settles.'

Modeen nodded and turned to Wolf. 'I guess you'll be going back to WA tomorrow?'

'Yep,' he drawled, 'I've got some packing to do.'

'Packing?' Noticing the gleam in his dark eyes and the grin twitching the corners of his lips, she frowned at him quizzically.

He gave up trying to hold back the smile. 'Seems I'm going to be relocating to Canberra.'

Spooky too was grinning and piped up, 'That's right. I thought if I have to move, I may as well make it worthwhile, so the Wolfman is taking up my post and I'm moving over to WA.'

Modeen's eyes lit up but her frown remained. 'I thought you loved Canberra, Spook?'

'I do, but a change is as good as a holiday, or so they say. And I've always wanted to see more of WA.'

He threw her a wink. 'Besides, it didn't take much to convince the Wolfman to move closer to—'

He hesitated before finishing with, 'Over here.'

Beside him Modeen and Wolf exchanged warm glances and then smiled into their drinks.

They had just been served their coffees when Ben gave a roll of his eyes and lowered his head, muttering, 'I'm beginning to think we're magnets for trouble.'

The others turned to see what was causing his angst and saw a dark-skinned man in a turban and flowing robes standing by the counter. The man had pulled a pump action shotgun from beneath his robes and whipped around to lock the café door. He waved the shotgun in the air and screeched at the clientele to, 'Sit down on the floor, with your backs to the front door … NOW!'

Most of the shocked customers were on their feet. Some screamed and cried out when he used the gun to shepherd them to the floor.

As Bugs reached inside his leather jacket, Modeen held up a hand at him and said, 'I've got this.' Sculling her coffee, she rose to her feet. 'Meet you back at HQ.'

Dressed in civvies, she blended with the café crowd in her blue jeans and white T-shirt. Moving with an innocent air, she walked up behind the man at the counter. When he whirled to face her, she smiled sweetly at him.

His lip curled and he yelled, 'You ignorant bitch! Get over with the others.' Holding the shotgun across his chest, he went to shove her away.

She stepped back saying smoothly, 'That's not a left-handed shotgun, you know. You're holding it the wrong way.'

When he frowned and looked down at the weapon, she stepped in and put her hand over his that was clutching the gun's fore-end. Before he could react, she swiftly placed her other palm against the end of the stock and pumped the weapon, tilting it a fraction as she did so.

It responded as it was designed to do, by ejecting a cartridge from the breach. It flew up to smack the man squarely on the nose.

When he screwed up his face and threw his head back, his grip on the weapon eased and Modeen promptly yanked it out of his grasp.

With a furious bellow he made to grab it back, as she lowered the butt and tapped it between his legs. His knees buckled and he reeled forward in pain.

She took a step back and swung the gun upward again, this time soundly collecting him under the chin with the flat side of the butt. His head snapped back and he fell against the counter before sliding to the floor, unconscious.

Modeen coolly pumped the weapon until all the cartridges had been ejected and then she handed it across the counter to the café manager, who was staring at her open-mouthed and dumbfounded. While most of the customers merely stood stunned, one of the men standing close to the counter gave the would-be terrorist a hearty kick in the stomach.

With a casual, 'I'd call the police if I were you,' to the manager, Modeen pushed her way to the front door past the cheering and clapping clientele. Unlocking the door, she stepped out onto the footpath and melted into the city crowds.

------

*If you've enjoyed **Modeen: Black Ops** I hope you'll consider submitting a review on your retailer's site and/or on Goodreads. And don't miss Modeen's next thrilling adventures in the following instalments.*

FHJ

OTHER BOOKS IN THE SERIES

THE MODEEN TRANSFORMATION

The 2nd action-filled Modeen adventure

Australian security agencies are on alert in the lead-up to the 2014 international G20 Summit being held in Brisbane, Queensland. Although aware of an increase in web activity on the summit site and into the backgrounds of its attending diplomats, even NatSec intel can't know what the terrorist group known as 'The Spear of Allah' is planning.

Something ex-SASR soldier and now NatSec agent, Jo Modeen, is about to find out in a very personal way....

MODEEN CONVERGENCE

The 4th Modeen high-action thriller

For the premier's planned visit to Cairns in far north Queensland, the Feds call on national security agency NatSec to provide assistance with the protection detail. Agent Jo Modeen is assigned the task, what she considers to be a 'babysitting' job ... until an attempt is made on her own life and it becomes clear the stakes are higher than first thought.
NatSec Beta Team leader Ben Logan re-forms Modeen's old unit, and they converge on what becomes a complex mission with dangerous links to the past....

MODEEN ROGUE

The 5th Modeen high-octane thriller

Decorated ex-special forces soldier and now national security agent Josephine Dakota Modeen struggles to come to terms with the fate of close teammate Troy 'Wolf' Wolverton. Critically injured during the team's most recent mission, he lies comatose in Brisbane Hospital's intensive care unit.
And the prognosis for his recovery isn't good.
Driven to pursue the organisation responsible, Modeen embarks on an unauthorised campaign of retribution.
A campaign that is both personal and perilous.

MODEEN REDEMPTION

The 6th Modeen adventure

In a high-tech Australian laboratory, final testing is underway of a deadly new prototype, a weapon that could alter the course of modern warfare and cement America's position as the world's dominant superpower.
The US Department of Defence is understandably anxious about security at the laboratory and tasks NatSec with providing additional on-ground surveillance.
No matter the cost, the prototype cannot be allowed to fall into the wrong hands....

MODEEN: FLASHPOINT

The 8th explosive adventure

When an LNG tanker is sunk in the Philippine Sea
north of Papua New Guinea, the spotlight falls on the
lucrative liquefied natural gas market. Believing an
international cartel to be responsible, and that
Australia's LNG plants could be at risk, the CIA tasks
NatSec with gathering on-site intel.
Modeen's team is deployed to discover the saboteurs'
identities, determine their next target, and find out just
how far they will go....

In *Modeen Convergence*, Modeen's team converges in far north Queensland on what becomes a complex mission with dangerous links to the past.

In *Modeen Rogue*, our heroine embarks on an unauthorised campaign of retribution. She's going rogue … and going alone.

In *Modeen Redemption*, NatSec is tasked with keeping safe the DOD's latest and most advanced weapon. A weapon that could alter the course of modern warfare, and must be kept secure at all costs….

The second box set is available as an ebook from your favourite online retailer.

THE JO MODEEN BOX SET: BOOKS 7-9

Due for release on 1 January, 2021

In *Modeen: Rules of Engagement,* Modeen and team find themselves defending honour and truth … and Ben's past actions.

In *Modeen: Flashpoint,* the sinking of an LNG tanker north of Papua New Guinea sees Modeen and team deployed to uncover those responsible, and determine what - or who - is the next intended target.

In *Modeen: Strikeforce,* British SAS and US Night Stalkers are deployed to Afghanistan to rescue pilots captured by the ruthless Red Group. It's an impressive strikeforce, but will it be enough?

The third box set is available as an ebook from your favourite online retailer.